be disappointed…it has everything in you can imagine: romance, adventure, mystery, and mayhem all rolled into one spectacular book!"
— Jessica Mitchell (Reader, Amazon Kindle)

"[BLACK MOON RISING] was holy wow."
— Starswarlover (Reader, Amazon Kindle)

"Ann Simas has struck gold [with BURIED TO DIE). It's a great read."
— Chuck Wallace, Reader (via Ann Simas Facebook page)

"I like everything about [FRUITYCAKES]. It gave me such a warm feeling and it also made me laugh."
— Annette (Reader, BookBub)

"Loved 'HERE AND GONE' couldn't hardly put it down, but my animals and husband needed to eat."
— Nora Levenhagen (Paperback Reader, Amazon)

"[HERE AND GONE] just pulls you in and you just keep reading and reading to find out what happens next."
— Jamie Kurp (via Candid Book Reviews)

"[HERE AND GONE] proves to be stuffed with danger and drama…[Ann Simas] has given her finest in this one keeping us engaged through every bit."
— Denise Van Plew (Reader, Amazon Kindle)

"Love, love, loved [HERE AND GONE]! Hoping for a sequel!"
— Gayle J. Brown (Reader, via Facebook)

"Death threats, crooked cops, sexual tension, dead bodies, crop circles and a cliff-hanger all wrapped up in a satisfying thriller [in QUILTED TO DIE]!"
— Kindle Reader (Reader, Amazon Kindle)

"You may need tissues for [ANGELS ON THE ROOFTOP]."
— Christine Campbell (Reader, Amazon Kindle)

"[DECK THE GNOMES] is a fun entertaining holiday romance that had me laughing out loud at times."
— Brenda M. (Reader, Amazon Kindle)

"BACK-DOOR SANTA is such a cute and funny romance novel. [Simas] has a way with her characters that I never really see that much in other books."
— Jessica Mitchell (Reader, Amazon Kindle)

"I loved, loved, loved [TAKEN TO DIE]! It took me a month to get started reading this book because I knew I wouldn't want It to end. I love the Grace Gabbiano series so much and can hardly wait for the next installment."
— cocogib (Reader, Amazon Kindle)

"[In JINGLE BELL CLOCK] there's magic in the air and a mystery to be solved!"
— Emily Pennington (Reader, Amazon Kindle)

"[REINDEER BLITZ is] something a little bit different but very entertaining. A perfect festive treat to curl up with.
— Amanda (UK Reader, Amazon Kindle)

"You are not going to want to put this book down! DISAPPEARING ACT is a page turner from the beginning of the story until the happily-ever-after at the end."
— hmg_vermont (Reader, Amazon Kindle)

Books by Ann Simas...

Afterstories
Chloe's Spirit[†]
Chloe's Spirit Afterstories
First Star[†]
First Star Afterstories

Stand-Alones
Blessed Are the Eagles[†]
Loose Ends
Heaven Sent
Black Moon Rising

Fossil, Colorado Series
Here and Gone
Disappearing Act
Run or Don't *(coming 2021)*

Grace Gabbiano Mysteries
Dressed to Die
Sliced to Die
Buried to Die
Quilted to Die
Taken To Die
Praying to Die
Framed to Die *(coming July 2021)*

Andi Comstock Supernatural Mysteries
Holy Smoke
Penitence
Angel Babies
Hellfire
The Wrong Wicca

Christmas Valley Romances
Santa's Helper
Candy Cane Lane
Let It Snow
FruityCakes
Sleigh Bride
Angels on the Rooftop
Deck the Gnomes
Back-Door Santa
Jingle Bell Clock
Reindeer Blitz
Holly Jollies

Short Story Collection
All's Well

[†]RWA Golden Heart Finalists

HOLLY JOLLIES

ANN SIMAS

MAGIC
MOON
PRESS

HOLLY JOLLIES

November 2020

ISBN 978-1-7347255-3-7 (print book)

Magic Moon Press . POB 41634 . Eugene, OR 97404-0386

Editing by Nancy Jankow

Printed in U.S.A.
103020/12pthyph
KP 734725537

Have a holly jolly Christmas.
It's the best time of the year.
I don't know if there'll be snow,
But have a cup of cheer.
— Johnny Marks

It is Christmas in the heart
that puts Christmas in the air.
— W.T. Ellis

Chapter 1

Holly Morgan misplaced her Christmas spirit sometime around age eleven, when her mother decided to enter her in a beauty contest.

Almost twenty years later, that pageant had faded into oblivion, but sometimes, it seemed like just yesterday that she still believed in Santa Claus.

Somehow, she had to find her Christmas spirit again. She was convinced that when she did, her life would be complete and she'd be back to normal. No longer would she be a walking shell who didn't care about anything or anybody. She'd have a real tree, with real Christmas decorations, and real presents beneath it.

So what if she was all alone, and all the presents would be from Holly to Holly, and her Christmas dinner would be eaten at a beautifully set table with her as the lone diner?

By the time she'd graduated from high school, she'd already become an established model—again, thanks to her mother. The media had slurped up her mother's suggestion that she be dubbed Sophisti-Kitty, because every successful teenage model needed a snappy pseudonym, after all. The downside was that it also sent a message to men that she could purr on sight.

Holly hated the moniker from the beginning, and she never purred. Not about anything. To this day, she wondered why her mother hadn't named her Kitty from the get-go. Maybe then, she would've been used to it and adding Sophisti to the front of it wouldn't have bothered her so much.

Along with nickname came blonde hair and blue eyes. Thanks to hair bleach and contact lenses, her mother's younger alter ego was created. Holly had also become reed slim. Until a few months earlier, she couldn't remember the last time she'd feasted on a good ole American hamburger. With fries. And a chocolate shake.

Nineteen years. She couldn't believe she'd let her mother push her around and schedule her life, even after she'd turned eighteen. From beauty pageants, to the modeling competition, to facing cameras almost on a daily basis all around the world, her life had been a nightmare. She'd considered swallowing herself into oblivion with booze or drugs, but it was much easier and less painful to show up for work and hide out afterward.

If she ever had to smile for a camera again, or force her body into another unnatural pose, Holly thought she might puke. She hated cameras. She hated the media. She hated magazines and TV ads. She even hated the way her mother had soaked up the limelight like a thirsty, greedy sponge.

Six months earlier, her mother had collapsed and died of a heart attack. A dedicated health freak, Constance had exercised daily and eaten only "healthy" foods. She'd also drunk to excess, smoked more than two packs a day, and popped uppers and downers, depending on her schedule, like they were candy.

Holly had long ago given up bickering with Constance about her over-abundance of bad habits cancelling out her supposed healthy habits. Why bother, when her mother refused to listen to any advice that didn't involve her daughter's finances, and didn't come from a man?

Holly wasn't sure when she'd stopped loving her mother. All she knew for certain was that it had been long enough ago that she no longer felt guilty about it.

There was a time when she'd recognized that mothers and daughters could be best friends, but she'd never had that with her mother. Instead, she got constant nagging, belittling, and push-push-pushing to make more of herself. In retrospect, she would've given anything to have a normal relationship with a normal mother, but it was too late to cry over spilt milk.

The day after her mother's funeral, Holly traded her Lexus LC500 Sport Coupe in for a more practical Honda CR-V. She also bought a golden retriever puppy, something she'd been wanting since she was eight. She stopped at PetSmart on the way home to buy dog supplies, and after she walked Blaze around the inside of her house, she had a good, long talk with the puppy about what she expected.

In response, Blaze licked her face, wagged his tail, and puppy *yipped* at her.

Holly was convinced they'd get along famously. "Remember, no peeing on the floor. You gotta go, bark and I'll let you out."

Blaze promptly peed on the floor.

Holly laughed and cleaned up the mess. One of the things she'd promised herself was that she *wouldn't*, under any circumstances, be like her mother. Ever.

It had taken all of those six months for her to put some meat on her bones and she liked the result.

Three months in, she had finally figured out what she wanted to do with the rest of her life. Her contract was nearly up with the modeling agency and she had no intention of signing a renewal. She hated modeling, but she loved drawing, and she had a talent for it. She applied to a publishing company looking for someone who was willing to work remotely on nonfiction projects. She sent them JPGs of some of her work and they hired her. The salary wasn't great, but God knows, she didn't need the money, and she'd be free to work from home, wherever that was.

A month after that, she bought a U.S. Atlas and began her search for a place to live, keeping in mind that she was looking for a location that would help bring back her Christmas spirit. She couldn't believe it when, after days of searching, she came across Christmas Valley. Who knew there were towns with *Christmas* in the name?

The atlas told her nothing about the place, so she did an online search and discovered it was a small burg, nestled in a valley near the mountains. That left Holly with a good feeling. Even though the town wasn't large, it still had a train station, an airport, and snow. Lots of snow.

The mountains and the snow did it for her. Despite her mother's protestations, she'd always accepted jobs in the mountains and snow country. She wasn't allowed to get out and play in the fluffy white stuff, but being able to breathe fresh mountain air, and to sit and enjoy looking at the landscape, always gave her a feeling of contentment. Holly knew she was born to be a mountain girl.

Once she had the location of her new home settled, she went through her closet and packed her new every-day clothes and shoes, and several pieces of jewelry that she actually liked, but had never been allowed to wear. She set those two bags aside just as the doorbell rang. With any luck, the estate-sales agent had arrived.

A few minutes later, she told the man, whose name was Abercrombie Jones, "I want to sell everything,"

"Everything?"

"Everything."

He practically gaped as he glanced around at his surroundings. "Are you sure?"

"Positive." Holly didn't care about anything in the house. Her mother had taken over decorating it in her style, not Holly's. She wasn't sure yet what her style actually was, but when she got to her new town, she'd find out. "You're welcome to work with the real estate agent, Lizzie Carrington. She plans to put up the for-sale sign the day after tomorrow. If you're amenable, she's interested in having everything remain in place. She's says a furnished place that looks lived-in shows better and should help sell the house more quickly."

"She's right about that." He looked around again. "So...are you thinking the estate sale can happen once the house is sold?"

"Lizzie and I would like the estate sale to happen four days before closing. She'll bring in cleaners two days before closing, when everything is gone."

He nodded. "I like that idea. You have this well-planned." He looked around again. "And everything is top quality. I'm sure we'll have no trouble selling what's here."

"Including the clothing I leave hanging in the closet."

After a slight hesitation, he nodded.

"If you have to do a reduced-price sale on the second afternoon, go for it. I don't care about the money."

That seemed to startle him, but he didn't comment or ask why. "Where will you be while this is happening?"

"Gone."

"Gone? I'm sorry. I don't know what that means."

"That's as it should be, Mr. Jones. Please contact Regina Freeman, my attorney, if you need anything. She's in charge of any financial matters."

"I see." He didn't question Holly further. Maybe that meant he'd dealt with stranger people than her before.

After he left, she went to the bathroom and pulled her hair into a ponytail, which took some doing, because it hung midway down her back. She then proceeded to whack off her hair three inches past the fabric-covered rubber band. Once that was done, she opened the box of hair dye that matched her dark roots and dyed her hair.

While the timer ticked down the minutes the dye needed to work, she used cotton balls and polish remover to take the polish off her fingernails. With a few minutes left, she used the nail clippers to trim her nails short, then gave them a quick filing.

Sans long blonde hair and ridiculously long fingernails, she felt one hundred percent freer until she looked at herself in the mirror.

It was strange seeing her reflection with dark hair again, and she was reminded that she'd forgotten to take out the blue contact lenses. They had no prescription attached to them, but her mother had insisted that blue eyes went better with blonde hair than did green eyes.

Holly removed the lenses and tossed them into the wastebasket, along with all the paraphernalia that went with contact lenses, including the spare pair. She was happy to have her green eyes back, and half an hour later, she dried her hair, amazed that it now had a little curl to it that helped mask her rudimentary cut.

She loaded up her car, then went back inside and checked once more that she had everything she wanted from the house. Satisfied, she headed to her bedroom with Blaze skittering along on the marble floor beside her.

That night, as she readied for bed, she was almost sorry she'd bought the CR-V. It would have been fun to take the train across the country to Christmas Valley, but given that she still had a practical side, she knew she'd need transportation when she got to where she was going, plus, she also had Blaze now, and riding in a crate on a train wouldn't be fair to him.

She calculated it would take four days to make her journey. Of course, that would change if she discovered any sights she wanted to see along the way, or if she ran into bad weather, or if her new SUV gave her problems.

Holly didn't mind. She had no timetable to stick to, no appointments to keep, no early morning modeling calls to make. She had a new phone, too, and the only numbers she'd plugged into CONTACTS were her attorney, the real estate agent, and the estate-sales agent.

The next morning, she was up at six a.m. and on the road by seven. Three hours later, she topped off her gas tank and took Blaze for a short walk. Bless his little puppy heart, he was doing well riding in the crate. After that, she hit a drive-thru for a breakfast sandwich and a cup of coffee before she got back on the road again.

Excitement burbled up inside her. A few more days and she'd be in Christmas Valley.

Her brand new life was off to a good start.

Rufus and Dinah

Dinah, the guardian angel assigned to Holly Morgan, and Rufus, the guardian angel assigned to Asher Hammell, stood in the driveway of Holly's sprawling Frank Lloyd Wright-style home. Both were frowning.

"Are we handling this properly?" Dinah asked.

"The girl hasn't had any Christmas spirit for almost twenty years," Rufus reminded her. "Christmas is a time of giving and sharing and loving. Who better to do that with than Ash's son, Hank?"

"She might not take to children."

"You of all people know that's not true," Rufus said in a censuring tone.

"I don't mean to be obtuse, Rufus, but just because Holly was pregnant doesn't mean she likes children."

"I have it on good authority" —he pointed skyward— "that before we took over her guardian angelship, she was in a funk for a long time over losing that baby."

"Funk? Since when did you start using pop-culture verbiage?"

He grinned at her. "Since I started hanging around with you so much."

Dinah didn't bother to reply. Her mind was on Holly. If the place they were steering her to was really the *right* place for her to be, everything would be hunky-dory. Christmas Valley was lovely, and it was full of nice people.

However, just because it had *Christmas* in the name didn't mean it was going to get Holly out of her *funk*.

Chapter 2

Asher Hammell sat on the floor beside the tub, watching his son play Rubber Ducky meets Sandy Submarine. So far, Rubber Ducky had the upper hand.

"Daddy," Hank said, smiling up at him, "pwease hand me the whao."

Ash obliged his son, who had been named Henry, after his father-in-law, but went by Hank. "You want the shark, too?"

Hank frowned, thinking. "Not yet."

"Play time is almost over," Ash said. "We have another big day ahead of us tomorrow."

"But not in the woods."

"No, not in the woods."

"Didn't get dirty today wike when I pwayed in the mud." He offered that up with an impish grin.

Ash grinned back. "No, you sure didn't."

"'Cuz there was snow."

"That's right."

"Can I take my bath toys out in the snow tomorrow?"

"Maybe."

That seemed to satisfy Hank. "I'm ready for Mary."

Ash handed over Mary Mermaid.

His son aimed her at Sandy Submarine and hit his mark.

There had been a time, right after Alicia's accident, when Ash thought he'd never be able to parent alone. Hell, who was he kidding? Some days, when he'd been out on search-and-rescue, he wasn't being a parent, anyway. On the day Alicia had died, she hadn't been a parent, either, but she had been a cheater, and Ash, being away from home so much, had never even noticed.

Alicia and her boyfriend had stolen away for a weekend at a nearby ski resort. She'd told Ash her book club had chosen the spot for their annual getaway, and he hadn't questioned it. Alicia had lined up a babysitter, who happened to be Kenzie, the cousin of Ryker Manning, a friend of his. Ryker vouched for Kenzie, and that was good enough for Ash.

Later, he had to wonder how Alicia had time to find a boyfriend, when she was supposedly with Hank all day. In retrospect, he should have noticed that the house was no longer neat and tidy when he rolled in every night, half-dead from working two jobs every day.

Going through the books a month after her death, he finally figured it out. Mark Lymon had installed the whole-house audio system. At the same time, he'd also installed himself into Alicia's life. Was it any wonder one-year-old Hank used to ask him, "Where Da-Da?" His son had seen more of Mark in those days than he had his own father.

Ash had regrets about that. If only he'd been a better husband. If only he'd been a better father. If only he didn't know Alicia had started her affair with Mark Lymon six months after Hank was born. If only she hadn't snuck away for a weekend and gotten herself killed riding a snowmobile with her bastard boyfriend who had inadvertently steered the machine into a boulder. If only.

Two months after Alicia's death, Ryker had given himself a stern talking-to. Basically, it amounted to straighten-up-and-fly-right-because-you-have-a-kid-who-needs-you. No more if-onlys were allowed. Period.

Ash had taken that lecture to heart. Hank needed him. But, how was a former Navy SEAL, who'd never changed a diaper, supposed to know *how* to take care of an almost one-year-old who was learning how to walk, and talk, and had his hands free to create what amounted to a small mountain of chaos?

Ryker had suggested he contact his wife's best friend, Lily D'Arcy, who was married to their mutual friend, Sean. At the time, she and Sean had been married for a year and she was expecting. They also had a three-year-old daughter, Macey, from Lily's previous marriage. "Lily will teach you what you need to know," Ryker had assured him, and sure enough, Lily did exactly that. She also taught him the basics of cooking and how to do the laundry, and suggested ways to keep the house neat and tidy. Lily was one of those people who could accomplish a thirty-six-hour day in twenty-four hours.

Some days, Ash couldn't believe how much work went into to being a single parent. It wasn't just the time and energy, it was also the amount of effort and coordination parenting took. His new business, Mountain Search-and-Rescue, which gave him one job to focus on instead of two, seemed tame by comparison. Of course, Lily had three years of practice as a single mom under her belt, but even so, Ash was pretty sure it was just the way God made Lily to begin with.

"I'm ready for the shark, Daddy."

Ash picked up the bathtub shark and dropped it in the water, which always made Hank laugh.

His son grabbed the rubber predator and crashed him into Willy Whale. "Yay!" Hank shouted.

Water splashed everywhere from the resulting battle, but Ash didn't mind getting wet. It was a small part of their daily routine, and it made him happy to know that Hank was happy.

"Going on my tummy, Daddy!"

"Okay, but be careful." Hank had taken swimming lessons over the summer, but a swimming pool was a lot different than a bathtub. As a certified EMT, Ash knew better than most how dangerous a bathtub could be.

Disregarding his father's warning, Hank resituated himself so that he was on his belly and began to kick the water, like he was a frogman. "Is this how you did it, Daddy?"

"Sort of," Ash said, then cautioned, "You don't have to kick quite so hard."

Hank grinned up at him and reduced his speed.

"That's better."

The doorbell sounded.

"Someone's here!" Hank squealed, back on his bottom so fast it made Ash's head spin. "Who is it?"

"I don't know. We're not expecting company are we?"

Hank's eyes widened. "No."

"Good thing we gave you a good scrubbing before you had playtime."

Hank nodded, his expression serious. "Good thing."

Ash lifted his son out of the bathtub and set him down on the bathmat before wrapping a towel around him.

The doorbell rang again.

"Hurry, Daddy."

Ash lowered the trip lever and the tub began to drain. He picked up the bath toys and dropped them into the caddy before he scooped up his son and headed for the front door.

He pulled it open, but no one was there. Thinking

someone was playing Ding-Dong Ditch, he started to close the door, then realized someone was headed down the walkway. "Can I help you with something?" he called out.

The person turned, but he couldn't get any particulars about who it was, since he hadn't turned on the porch light.

"I'm sorry to bother you," a voice came back, "but I seem to be lost. I'm looking for the Hammell place."

"You found it." He hesitated, wanting to get a better look at whoever belonged to that voice, and why was the sound of it doing something strange to his insides? "I need to get my son dried and into his jammies."

She remained where she was, still and silent.

Ash couldn't blame her. He hadn't meant to respond so gruffly, but too late to call back the tone of his voice. "Be right back." He closed the door part way and headed for Hank's room.

"Who's that wady?" Hank asked.

"I have no idea."

"Maybe she wants the wittow house."

"You know, buddy, I think you might be right." For some reason, Ash hadn't considered that anyone would come knocking on his door at seven o'clock about the cottage he had for rent. He dried Hank quickly and got him into his PJs. Together, they hurried back to the entryway, where they found the door closed.

Ash opened it to see if the visitor had taken off and found her with her arms wrapped around her waist, shivering. "Why didn't you come inside?"

"You didn't invite me in."

He opened his mouth to rebut, but realized she was right. He'd been so concerned about Hank catching a chill, he hadn't asked her to come in. It was courteous of her to close the door, but didn't she have enough sense to come in out of the cold, even if he hadn't invited her in?

He peered past her, looking for her car. "Where's your vehicle?"

"Off the road, about a mile that way."

She pointed toward the east, which told him nothing.

"Actually, I'm not sure it's actually a mile, but it certainly felt like it while I was walking."

"Why didn't you call a tow truck?"

"I tried, but I couldn't get phone reception."

Of course, she couldn't. Half the time out here, he couldn't either, which was why he also had a land line.

"Are you Asher Hammell?" she asked, her teeth rattling against each other.

"Yes," he responded in a curt tone, then wondered what the hell was wrong with him.

Hank clung to his knee and stared at the stranger. That didn't, however, stop his son from raising his little hand in a wave. "Hi."

"Hello," she answered with a teeth-chattering smile. "What's your name?"

"Henry, but everybody caws me Hank."

"It's nice to meet you, Hank."

He nodded in lieu of answering, and then he did something amazing. He smiled.

Ash sucked in a breath. Over the past three years, no stranger had ever gotten a smile out of his son. He gave this particular stranger a second look. She had a knit cap pulled down low over her head, but her lightweight coat explained the teeth-chattering. She also wore no gloves, and the penny loafers on her feet were not the best choice for footwear in snowy weather.

Which reminded Ash that he still hadn't invited her inside. He stood back and said, "Please, come in."

"Th-th-thank y-y-you."

Her pathetic reply made him feel like a cretin, not to mention foolish. Angry with his inept response to her unexpected appearance, he slammed the door shut once she was inside, which made her jump. She lost her balance and teetered, but recovered before she toppled over.

"She needs hot chocwate, Daddy."

Ash nodded like an idiot.

The woman stared back at him with the greenest eyes he'd ever seen.

He couldn't tell if she was afraid of him, or if something else was going on. "Wait here. I'll bring you something hot to drink."

"Okay."

He turned and headed for the kitchen, but didn't realize Hank was no longer attached to his knee until he reached for the box of hot chocolate packets. He headed back toward the entryway, but neither his son nor the woman were there. Ash's first thought was that she'd kidnapped his child. His head almost exploded over that, but he forced himself to remain calm.

And then he heard Hank and the stranger in the living room, talking. He moved over to the archway between the entry and living room and discovered them standing at the fireplace.

Hank parroted her, holding out his hands to let the flames warm them.

"This feels so good," the woman said.

Hank nodded. "Daddy ahways makes a big fire. You want a bwanket?"

"No, but thank you. The heat from the fire is warming me up just fine."

Great. Now his kid, who was not quite four, was a better host than he was.

The only excuse he had to offer was that the woman, whoever she was, had thrown a curve ball his way and he'd done a rotten job of dodging it.

Chapter 3

Holly moved a step closer to the fire, hoping to absorb more warmth. How stupid could she have been to take off walking to the nearest residence with only a denim jacket on over her sweater, no gloves, and wearing penny loafers? At least she'd had the foresight to pull on the knit cap she'd bought at the convenience store inside the gas station.

"Wanna howd Teddy? He keeps me warm."

Holly smiled down at the child. It had taken a moment, but she quickly figured out he had a problem pronouncing his Ls. "Thank you for offering, but you'd better hug him tight, if that's the case."

Hank picked up Teddy and swung him back-and-forth by the arm a couple of times, then clutched the bear to his chest. "He sweeps with me every night."

"I bet he likes that."

The boy nodded, his expression serious. "Do you have a Teddy to sweep with?"

"No, I have a dog, but he's not allowed on my bed."

His expression brightened. "Where is he?"

"On the porch."

"Our porch?"

Holly nodded. Had the little boy never seen a dog before?

Hank spun on his heel and ran for the front door. He had to drop the bear to use both hands to open it, and when he did, he whooped with joy. "A puppy!" he yelled.

Blaze was always happy to see people, but apparently, he was extra happy to see someone more his size.

Hank dropped to his knees and put his arms around the dog's neck. "I wuv him. What's his name?"

"Blaze."

"Why didn't you say you had a dog with you?" the boy's father demanded, picking up both the boy and the puppy. He used his booted foot to close the door, then brought the puppy and his son over to the fireplace and set them down.

Holly tried to explain herself, but nothing came out except, "I…."

"Good God, don't you have any common sense?" he practically snarled.

Startled by his anger, Holly took a step back and bumped into the hearth. She lost her balance, tried to recover, and failed. The back of her head smacked against the brick façade that ran all the way to the ceiling.

She saw stars just before everything went black.

Hank started crying the moment the woman fell backward.

Ash knew he was to blame for his son's reaction. He never yelled like that, and for the life of him, he didn't know why he'd yelled at someone he didn't even know.

He managed to grab her before she went all the way to the floor. "Don't cry, Hank. She's okay," Ash assured his son as he carried the woman to the sofa.

"She hitted her head. It hurts to hit your head." As if his father didn't already know, he added, "And she's freezing."

"Grab the throw from the easy chair," Ash said, hoping that would take his son's mind off the woman's injury and his father's idiocy. A moment later, Hank handed him the corner of the cotton throw. "Thanks, son."

"She needs hot chocwate, Daddy."

Ash checked her pulse. A little rapid, but not life-threatening. He turned to his son and picked him up, wiping his tears. "Let's go make some hot chocolate right now. You want marshmallows?"

Hank nodded. "I need Teddy, too."

Ash looked around for the bear.

"He's by the door."

Ash retrieved the bear and the three of them, followed by the puppy, headed to the kitchen.

Once Hank was assured his father had the hot chocolate under control, he grabbed the puppy's collar and dragged him back to the living room. "C'mon, Blaze."

It didn't escape Ash that his son could pronounce the L in Blaze just fine, but he didn't take time to speculate on why that was. Five minutes later, he carried a tray with three hot chocolates and a plate of cookies to the living room.

Hank sat on the floor looking like he'd lost his best friend.

"Where'd she go?" Ash asked.

"Back to her car. She told me to tew you something, but I forgot what it was, except for 'never mind.'"

Ash set the tray down and hurried to the front door. He pulled it open and bolted down the walk. Thanks to the nearly full moon, he located the woman and the puppy easily on the roadway. Considering she was injured, she'd made good time. Still, her gait wasn't fluid, which could mean she either didn't know how to walk in snow or she'd injured herself in the fall. Holy shit! What if she had a concussion? He cursed himself for not checking her pupils.

Even as he watched, she tripped over the dog and went face first into the snow bank at the side of the road. The puppy yelped, then puppy squeak-barked at her, like that would make her get up.

Hank called out from the open doorway. "Daddy?"

"Stay right where you are, Hank. I'll bring her back." Ash raced down the road. When he reached her, he rolled her over, then squatted so he could lift her more easily.

All the way back to the house, he didn't know if he was angrier at himself for being a dipshit, or at her for making foolish decisions. Belatedly, he remembered the puppy. He looked down, surprised to find Blaze trotting beside him. "Close the door," he said to his son.

Hank did so with more force than necessary.

Ash read his kid's message loud and clear as he carried the woman to the spare bedroom. He used his elbow to hit the light switch, which controlled the bedside lamps, and laid her down gently.

Just as gently, he lifted her eyelids. Her pupils looked to be of equal size. He blew out a sigh of relief.

"Is she sweeping?" Hank asked.

"Maybe. Or she might be unconscious."

"What does that mean?"

"Sometimes, people who get a bump on the head pass out."

"You mean wike when Sam went off the mountain?"

"Yes."

"Does it hurt to be uncon…whatever you said?"

"No." He looked down at his son. "Don't worry, Hank. She's going to be fine."

"What about Blaze?"

"What about him?"

"Maybe he wants to be on the bed with the wady."

"Dogs don't sleep on beds in this house."

"They don't?"

"No. Just people sleep on the beds."

"Oh. The wady doesn't wet Blaze on her bed, either." Hank appeared to think about that for a moment. "Can I way down next to him?"

"No, you need to get into your own bed."

Hank scrunched up his face. "But she might need me."

"If she needs someone, I'll be here."

"You gonna way down with her?"

"No, I'm going to sit in the chair and watch her, in case she needs something."

"What if I bring my sweeping bag in here?"

Leave it to Hank to have a ready alternative. "Go get it and I'll get the hot chocolate. Be quiet, though."

His son nodded and tiptoed out of the room. Blaze pranced along at his heels.

Ash looked down at the woman one more time, then gently eased the knit cap off her head. A tumble of dark waves popped out. He reached out to touch them, then snatched his hand back. "Get a grip," he muttered, and contrary to what he'd just told his son, stomped out of the room, making enough noise to raise the dead.

Holly awoke in a room bathed in a soft light. She blinked several times, but had no recollection of how she'd gotten there. She pushed up on her elbows, surprised to find herself fully dressed, though her knit cap and her penny loafers had been removed. She also had a blanket draped over her.

She glanced around and noticed the homeowner, Asher

Hammell, sound asleep in the chair. As quietly as possible she threw off the blanket and eased her legs over the side of the bed, almost stepping on the boy in the dinosaur-print sleeping bag on the floor. Blaze was snuggled up next to him. Both were sound asleep.

She stepped over the sleeping bag without waking either of them and went in search of a bathroom. When she came out, Asher Hammell stood waiting for her like a mountain of ill content, his arms akimbo, scowling.

"Why didn't you wake me?"

"I haven't had help going to the bathroom since I was a toddler," she shot back, wavering slightly on her feet.

He put out a hand to steady her.

An electric current shot through her body at the contact, even though there was a sweater between her skin and his big hand. Holly didn't know what to make of it. "May I have a glass of water, please?"

He grasped her upper arm and led her down the hall to the kitchen. "Sit."

"Please, don't talk to me like I'm Blaze."

"Please. Sit."

She sat, offering him a wry smile.

He stared at her for fully fifteen seconds before he turned away and headed to the sink, where he filled a glass with water. "You want ice?"

"No, thank you."

"Are you hungry?"

She drank half the glass before she answered. "A little."

"That's a good sign."

"A good sign of what?"

"That you didn't severely injure yourself either time you fell."

"Either time?"

He nodded. "You fell back against the fireplace and passed out for a few minutes, and when I went to make hot chocolate, you took off for your car. You tripped over your dog and went face-first into the snow."

She stared at him like he'd grown a second head. "I did?"

"Don't you remember?"

"No."

He frowned and bent to look into her eyes again. "Your pupils look okay. Do you have a headache?"

"Yes, and I have a bump on the back of my head."

Ash extended his hand and ran it gently over her skull. "That's a good-sized lump," he said with surprise. "Are you sick to your stomach?"

"No. Should I be?"

"I hope not."

"Are you a doctor, or something?"

"No, I own Mountain Search-and-Rescue and I'm a certified EMT."

"Oh."

"Would you like me to fix you something to eat?"

She frowned. "I don't want you to go to any trouble."

He shrugged. "My culinary skills are pretty much average, but I could scramble a couple of eggs or make you a sandwich, or even offer you some cookies."

"I'll take the cookies."

He smirked at that. "Cookies are not exactly nutritious."

"Maybe not, but I do love cookies and I've been without them for so long, I have a lot of catching up to do." She offered him another smile, and wondered why he got that deer-in-the-headlights look again.

Rufus and Dinah

Dinah sighed. "They're perfect together."

Rufus frowned. "I'm not so sure. Personally, I'm having second thoughts about them."

"Why?"

"Both of them have a bad experience behind them, and they have trust issues."

Impatient with her co-guardian angel, Dinah *harrumphed*. "If you weren't sure about them, why didn't you intercede before she sold everything she owned and took off driving across the country to Christmas Valley?"

"Men, even male angels, don't necessarily think in romantic terms."

"What's that got to do with anything?" Dinah demanded. "I've been with you on two other assignments in Christmas Valley, both of which turned out perfectly. I don't remember you having doubts about those."

"You have selective memory," Rufus replied a bit pompously. "If you will recall, Joss and Lachlan seemed like a lost cause to us, right up until the end, when they finally realized they couldn't live without each other."

Dinah rolled her eyes. "Thank goodness you don't write Hallmark movie scripts."

Rufus belly-laughed. "Maybe I should. It would mix things up a bit."

"Can we get back to the topic at hand, which is Holly and Ash?"

"You worry too much."

"And usually, you don't worry enough, Rufus. What's so different this time?"

Rufus grunted and instead of answering, took a long puff on the pipe he'd acquired someplace between Holly's old town and her new one.

"Did the Big Guy give you permission to smoke that pipe?"

"I don't recall that the Angel Book of Rules addresses smoking at all."

"I'm pretty sure it addresses smoking, alcohol, and drugs," Dinah chided, shaking her head. "You have always been one who marches to your own drummer, haven't you?"

"And proudly so." From his perch next to her on the roof of Asher Hammell's home, he stared down at the scene unfolding below. "They're having an instant attraction to each other."

"Of course, they are. That's why we're here."

"I'm not so sure about that."

"Rufus, stop beating a dead horse to death!"

"I'm not! It's just that their relationship might be speeding along a little too quickly. They should get to know each other first."

"You're certifiable, Rufus. You know that?"

"I am not!" he retorted, then asked in a calmer voice, "What do you see that I don't?"

"Sometimes a person just *knows*," Dinah shot back, "and that's all there is to it."

"FYI, we are guardian angels, not persons."

She gave him a look. "You know what I mean."

"I wish I had your confidence."

She slid him another look, this one meant to maim. "I wish you did, too."

Chapter 4

Ash was intensely curious about the woman sitting across from him. "You know my name—I go by Ash, by the way—but I don't know yours."

"Holly Morgan." She lowered her gaze and examined the plate of cookies with a serious expression. She chose the biggest one.

"You look vaguely familiar."

She froze for a moment, then dunked her cookie into her hot chocolate. "I get that all the time."

"You do?"

She nodded. "I must look like everyone's mother–sister–cousin."

"I doubt that," he said. Even though she wore no makeup and her hair was going every which way, she was stunning. He expected her to ask why he doubted her statement, but she seemed content to enjoy the chocolate chip cookie and her hot drink.

She looked up once, smiled again, then quickly dropped her gaze, like she'd done something wrong.

Was she embarrassed to be caught looking at him? Intrigued, Ash couldn't resist asking, "What's the matter?"

She seemed to flounder for a moment, then said, "I shouldn't be enjoying this cookie as much as I am."

"Why not?"

She looked back up, staring at him for a moment before her gaze began to dart around the room, as if searching for an escape route. "I'm not supposed to eat cookies."

"Are you diabetic?"

"No."

"Then I don't understand why you're not supposed to eat them. Everyone loves cookies." To prove his point, he took two from the plate and shoved half of one of them into his mouth.

"Cookies make you fat."

He grunted in disbelief. When she hung her head even more, he asked, "Who told you that?"

"My mother," she answered. Though she was obviously going for a neutral tone, her reply held a touch of bitterness.

That explained everything and nothing, so Ash decided to let it drop. Instead he asked, "Why were you looking for me?"

She met his gaze. "I bought a paper in town and saw an ad for a cottage for rent. I need a place to stay and I thought it would be a good spot to land while I get a feel for the area."

"Where are you from?"

"Southern California, then New York, then SoCal again, and some other places."

Talk about ambiguous. "Christmas Valley is a small place, comparatively speaking. Are you planning to stay, or are you just visiting?"

"Christmas Valley is going to be my forever home."

Something about the way she said it, in a slightly defiant tone, puzzled him. "Have you been here before?"

"No, I found it in the road atlas I bought at the bookstore."

"You moved to a new place based on finding it on a road atlas?"

"Yes." Her green eyes narrowed on him. "Is there something wrong with that?"

"Not if you like surprises, I suppose." He considered her for a moment, then went on. "Christmas Valley is no Big Apple and it has no beaches, if you don't count our lakes."

"That's what I'm banking on." She finished her hot chocolate, stood, and went to the sink, where she rinsed her cup. She turned and folded her hands in front of her. "I'll come back tomorrow and look at the cottage, if it's still available."

In case she didn't know what time it was, he said, "It's almost midnight."

"I know."

"You can't sleep in your car."

"I have a blanket in the back seat."

He laughed. "The temperature is hovering at thirty-two degrees. You'll freeze your tush off."

She glanced out the kitchen window. "Thirty-two degrees?"

He nodded.

"That does present a problem."

At least she knew how cold thirty-two degrees Fahrenheit was. "When you said before that your car was off the road, did you mean *off* the road?"

"I skidded and before I could correct, I was in the ditch." She shook her head and frowned again. "I swear, it was almost like someone else was in charge of my SUV instead of me."

"Did you have a few drinks in town?"

"I don't drink."

He took her at her word, especially since she looked both indignant and shocked that he would suggest she might have been hammered when she got behind the wheel of her vehicle. Ash sighed. That's what being called in on too many DUI-related crashes in the mountains did to a guy. Still, he couldn't send Holly Morgan back to a car in the ditch to spend the night. "You can sleep in the spare bedroom. In the morning, I'll call the towing service. While Junior gets your SUV back on the road, I'll give you a tour of the cottage."

"Is it on this property?"

"Yeah, it was used as an art studio by the last owner, who I bought the property from two years ago."

Her eyes lit up. "Really?"

Holly Morgan's response fascinated him, but he didn't take time to analyze it. "Yes, and Lily helped me spruce up everything."

"Lily?"

"She's a friend of mine."

"I see," she said. "The ad says it's furnished. I hope that's true, since I have no furniture."

He judged her to be near thirty. Shouldn't she at least have a bed and a dresser? "Did you have some at one time?"

"Yes."

"What happened to it?" Since it was curiosity that killed the cat, Ash was grateful he wasn't a feline.

"I sold it."

Though he wanted to ask why, he decided to save that question for another time. "Lily says the cottage is cozy."

"It sounds perfect."

"It—"

She cut him off by saying, "Thank you for the offer of your spare bedroom. I'm exhausted. I've been traveling for the last seven days and on the road since six this morning."

"That would wear anyone out."

Her gaze shot around the room again, finally connecting with his. "Goodnight."

"'Night." He watched in silence as she left the kitchen. Did she plan to let Hank sleep on the floor beside her bed, or would she come back and ask him to carry his son to his own bedroom?

He waited, but she didn't return. He rinsed his cup and the empty cookie plate and put everything into the dishwasher. With a last look around, he shut off the light, checked the fireplace and the front door, then moved down the hall. He listened at her doorway, then knocked gently. When she didn't answer, he opened it about six inches.

Hank and the puppy were still sound asleep on the floor and Holly Morgan was already fast asleep on top of the bed.

With a sigh, Ash decided he couldn't sleep in his own king-size bed when he had to keep an eye on her. In his book, after hitting her head twice, she fell into the at-risk category. He checked the thermostat and raised the temperature control two degrees.

He pulled off his boots and left them in the hallway outside the spare bedroom, then moved quietly around the bed. Before he sat down, he pulled the extra blanket at the foot of the bed up over her.

He couldn't get over how beautiful she was, but it was more than that. She'd been good with Hank and that said a lot about her as a person.

For a moment, he considered curling up next to her, then decided against it. He doubted that she was a woman who'd appreciate waking up to find a strange man lying next to her.

Come to think of it, other than how she treated Hank and her puppy, he didn't know what kind of woman she was at all. The moment the thought occurred to him, he realized it was ludicrous.

He knew exactly what kind of woman she was. Kids and dogs weren't drawn to people who didn't like them. Kids and dogs intuitively knew a good person from a bad person and Holly Morgan obviously fell into the former category.

Which, judging from his own response to her, was bad news for him.

Chapter 5

Holly found a short person staring at her when she opened her eyes.

"I thought you were never going to wake up," Hank said with a sweet smile.

She smiled back at him. "I'm glad I did. Good morning."

"G'morning. Daddy said your name is Holly. We gots some holly pwants in the yard. Why are you named after a pwant?"

"Are you sure the plants aren't named after me?"

The boy thought about that for a minute, then shook his head. "It they named a pwant after you, it would be a lot prettier."

"Thank you, Hank. That's the nicest thing anyone's ever said to me."

"It is?"

She nodded.

His eyes brightened.

"Did you have a good sleep?"

His smile widened into a grin. "Blaze kept me company awo night."

"I bet he did."

"Did you have a good sweep?"

"I did, and I can't remember the last time I slept so well," she admitted.

"Daddy's fixing pancakes for breakfast. Do you wike pancakes?"

"That was my favorite breakfast when I was your age."

"How owd are you now?"

"Almost thirty."

His eyes widened. "That's reawy owd."

"Not *that* old," she replied with a smile. "Where's Blaze?"

"Watching Daddy make the pancakes. What does Blaze eat for breakfast?"

"He has dog food, but it's in the car. Want to take a walk with me after we eat to get it?"

"Maybe." He glanced down at her shoes. "You don't got any snow boots."

That's what happened when you did modeling shoots in snow country, but weren't allowed to venture outside to play in the snow. You forgot to buy snow boots. "Maybe your dad can give us a ride to my car."

"You ever been in a truck afore?"

Had she? If she had, she couldn't remember it. "I don't think so. Is it fun?"

"I haf'ta ride in the back seat, 'cuz I'm too short to ride in the front."

"I'm sorry to hear that."

"It's okay," he assured her. "I got a booster seat, and I get to see wot'sa stuff, wike bears and wions."

"Bears and lions," Holly teased, pretending to be afraid. "Are you sure?"

"Wewo, no, but when we see the reindeer, I pretend they're bears and wions."

"Reindeer?"

"Yeah, you know. For Santa's sweigh at Christmas."

"Who owns the reindeer?"

"Santa! Don't you know that?

She grinned at him and tapped his nose. "Honestly, I didn't know. I lost my Christmas spirit a long time ago." She hesitated. "Want to know a secret?"

He nodded, his expression solemn.

"That's why I came to Christmas Valley. I'm hoping to get my Christmas spirit back."

He stared at her with even wider eyes. "If you don't got Christmas spirit does that mean you don't get presents?"

She nodded.

Hank scrambled up on the bed and threw his arms around her neck, hugging her tight. "I'm sorry you wost your Christmas spirit, Holly."

Holly hugged him back, enjoying the feel of his arms around her and his sturdy little body next to hers. She looked up and found Ash Hammell standing in the doorway, watching them. He wore a curious expression she couldn't quite define.

"Breakfast is ready, you two," he said. "I left a toothbrush on the bathroom vanity for you, Holly." He turned and walked away without another word.

Hank followed her into the bathroom and watched with interest as she brushed her teeth, but she shooed him out when it was time to relieve herself. He scooted off toward the kitchen singing his version of "Frosty the Snowman."

His voice was so sweet and unrestrained, it almost made Holly cry.

Holly was impressed with the way Ash cooked. For

one thing, he cleaned up as he went. For another, he made the best pancakes she'd ever tasted.

She ate one more than she should've and three link sausages. She even snuck a sausage to Blaze, who sat beside her chair and let her know he was starving.

"You shouldn't give dogs table food," Ash said.

"I know, but I can't eat in front of him when he's hungry."

Ash shook his head and moved on to another topic. "The tow truck will be here around eleven."

Holly glanced at her watch. It was just after ten.

"I'll walk you out to the cottage and you can have a look around while I clean up the kitchen."

"I should do clean-up since you cooked."

"I'll take a rain check on that."

"Okay." A rain check, huh? That implied they'd have a future meal together. The possibility caused her insides to flutter. She polished off her milk and winked at Hank, who picked up his glass and did the same.

"Can I go to the cottage with Holly?" the boy asked his father.

Ash hesitated. "If it's okay with Holly."

Hank turned pleading eyes on her. "Can I?"

"Sure. You can be in charge of watching Blaze."

"Wow!" Hank said. "Thanks, Holly."

After breakfast, Ash led her, Hank, and Blaze down the freshly shoveled walkway. The lot was large and the cottage was situated about two hundred feet away from the main house.

Holly fell in love with it the moment she saw it. Even though she'd spent almost twenty years of her life being told what to do and how to do it, she knew in an instant the cottage was exactly what she'd hoped to find. It was straight out of the English countryside, with its stone façade, window boxes, and slate roof. It also had a rounded door top, which sealed the deal for her.

Ash inserted the key and unlocked that charming door. He opened it and stood aside so she and her two companions could enter.

She smiled up and him and said, "Thank you."

He nodded with a grim expression. "We should leave here at about ten-fifty, in case the tow arrives early."

"Okay." She smiled down at Hank. "You can be my tour guide."

"What does that mean?" the boy asked.

"You can show me where everything is."

He got a worried expression on his face. "I don't know where everything is. Maybe you should stay, Daddy."

"Don't worry, Hank," she said, hoping to reassure him. "We'll explore together." She glanced at Ash and found him studying her intently. "See you at ten 'til."

He nodded and flexed his jaw, as if he weren't certain about leaving her alone. Or was he worried about leaving her alone with his son?

Holly smiled at him and took Hank's hand. "We'll have to hurry, if we want to see everything."

"'Bye, Daddy!" Hank said with a grin, waving at his father.

Blaze puppy *yipped*, wagging his tail as he pranced around.

Ash pulled the door closed and headed back to the main house.

Holly turned in a circle, taking in everything. She'd always dreamed about living in a little place like this. Furnished with antiques, it wasn't over-full with them. There were Art Deco prints on the wall, which happened to be a favorite period of hers. They wandered through to the kitchen, which was big enough to hold a pine table with six chairs. The cabinets were a shaker-style, painted a taupe color, and had tiny forks and spoons for knobs. It also had a dishwasher, but even if it hadn't, Holly would have been in love with the room. There was even a shelf holding a variety of cookbooks.

She opened the cupboards, happy to note she wouldn't have to buy dishes or pans or serving pieces or silverware. Obviously, there were no food-stuffs, but that was easily remedied. "This is a great kitchen," she said to Hank who stuck with her as she explored.

"You gonna 'vite us to dinner?" he asked.

"If your dad agrees to rent to me, I sure will," she assured him. "What's your favorite food?"

"Sketti," he replied promptly.

"I love sketti, too," she said, grinning.

They went next to the main bedroom, which held a king-size bed. It was way bigger than she needed, but even so, it brought an unbidden image of her and Ash in that bed together.

Holly felt her face flush. She'd only had one boyfriend and she'd ended up marrying him when she turned up pregnant after having sex once. The second time had been on their wedding night. After that, he informed her he couldn't stand looking at her pregnant belly. He'd made no secret of how many other women he had sex with who had sense enough *not* to get pregnant.

The marriage had lasted three months, but it had taught Holly a valuable lesson. Well, two really. Always use birth control and never marry a man who didn't make your heart sing, because somehow, he'd use it against you.

She opened the closet and discovered it was a walk-in with lots of shelves and drawers, in addition to hanging rods. "Perfect," she murmured. The bedroom also had a large window with a beautiful view of the mountains.

"The big mountain is Mount Beady," Hank informed her. "Daddy has to go up there and rescue peepoe."

"He does, does he?"

Hank's head went up-and-down. "Sometimes peepoe don't pay 'tention to what they're doing."

From the horse's mouth to his little pony's. "They're lucky your Daddy can help them."

"I know. Mommy died on Mount Beady."

That brought Holly up short. "She did? I'm so sorry, Hank."

"I never knowed her, 'cuz I was a baby when she died. She's in heaven now."

"How old are you?" she asked the little sage.

"Awmost four," he said, holding up four fingers. "My birthday is two days afore Christmas."

"So's mine," Holly said. "What a coincidence."

"What's a coincidence?" he asked her.

"It means we both have a birthday on the same day. We'll have to celebrate together."

"Can you bake me a SpongeBob SquarePants cake?"

Startled, Holly said, "I can sure try."

He hugged her legs. "I'm happy you're here, Holly. And Blaze, too."

They finished the tour of the cottage, which also consisted of a large bathroom and the large spare room that was a fully equipped artist's studio, complete with a fireplace. Not that Holly needed all the art supplies, since she had her own, but it might be fun to try her hand at something different.

"You gonna rent this cottage?" Hank asked, sitting down to pet Blaze.

"I hope so, because I love it." Holly more than loved it, but how did she explain that to an almost four-year-old? She realized belatedly that she should temper her response, in case Hank's dad didn't think she'd be a suitable renter. "Whether I do rent or not," she said, "depends on if your dad decides I'll be a good tenant."

"Tenant?"

"Renter."

He nodded. "Aunt Wiwwy and Daddy fixed up the cottage."

"Aunt Lily must be a good friend."

"She is and Unca Sean, too. Pwus, they gots kids I can pway with—Macey, Rian, Ronan, Kiernan, and Mary Kate, 'cept Mary Kate is stiwa baby and she doesn't know how to pway yet."

Holly felt a wave of relief that Lily and Ash weren't an item, but for the life of her, she didn't know why she cared.

Rufus and Dinah

Dinah hugged herself. "The cottage is a perfectly enchanting place for their romance to start."

"For the record, Dinah," Rufus said, "their romance started the minute Ash opened his front door to her."

"Do you always have to rain on my parade, Rufus?"

"I don't do it deliberately."

"I beg to differ. From my point-of-view, you do."

Rufus sighed. "I may rain on your parade, but you can *never* keep on topic. We're supposed to make sure Holly and Ash get together, are we not? How are we supposed to do that when you're constantly lecturing me about something?"

"I am not!"

"You are! And it's not just lecturing. You also argue with me about everything."

"You are so full of it, Rufus!"

He blustered for a moment. "I can't believe you just said that. The Angel Book of Rules is quite definite about profanities. It does *not* allow them."

"I said absolutely *nothing* profane. You can be so dense sometimes!"

"You just told me I'm full of it. What else would you call that, if not swearing?"

"I could have meant you're full of hot air…which you *are*."

Rufus focused on his original interpretation. "Ha! You meant cow dung and you know it."

Dinah sighed. "In all honesty, I didn't mean anything. It was simply a turn of phrase."

He gave his head an angry shake. "Sometimes I feel like strangling you."

She blustered. "So it's okay for you to threaten to kill me, but I can't utter a turn of phrase?"

"That's right!" he shot back without thinking.

"Sometimes, I feel like giving you a good shove off the roof." And with that proclamation, she raised her arms and gave him a heave-ho, which sent him sliding down the roof and into the snow below.

Chapter 6

Ash headed out to the cottage at ten forty-five. He stepped inside, wondering where Hank and Holly were. He found them in the garage. "Any questions?"

"Where's the snow shovel?" Holly asked.

"There isn't one. I take care of shoveling the walks."

"What if I want to take care of my own?"

"You can either buy one, or borrow the shovel in my garage."

She nodded. "I didn't notice a driveway, but since we're in the garage, I know there must be one."

"I'll have the snowplow stop by and clear it."

"Does that mean you're okay with renting to me?"

"How do you know you want to? You haven't asked about the rent yet."

At the risk of giving away her excitement, which might cause him to charge her an exorbitant rent, she said, "I love this place. It's exactly where I want to live for now."

He named a reasonable amount, which was hundreds

less than Holly had expected.

"That seems too low."

"Considering this is Christmas Valley, and rents here *are* low, it's actually higher than I wanted to charge, but it does include utilities," he informed her.

"That's not fair to you. I expect to reimburse you for those separately," she said.

"No need."

"Yes, there *is* a need. Either I reimburse them, or I can't rent from you."

Ash didn't like being challenged about a decision he'd already made, but he was willing to make a concession. "What if we have a set amount every month, which should average out over the course of a year?"

"How much?"

"A hundred."

"That's not enough."

"How do you know? Are you familiar with the cost of utilities here in the Valley?"

"Well, no, but—"

"Take it or leave it." Ash knew he might regret his ultimatum, but she was testing his patience.

"I'll take it, but I don't like the way you bargain."

In return, he offered her a smirk and a shrug. "Ready to go?"

"Piggy-back to the house, Daddy?" Hank asked, holding tight to Blaze.

"Only for you, son. Dogs don't get to go piggy-back."

Hank didn't appear to like the sound of that. "No piggy-back for me, then."

Ash watched as his son trudged back inside the cottage with the puppy half in his arms. "He's been begging me for a dog. I guess since he has yours, that discussion is over for the time being." He glanced down at Holly, surprised to find her staring after Hank with tears streaming down her cheeks. Before he could ask what was wrong, she swiped them away and dashed inside.

The tow driver arrived at exactly eleven o'clock. Ash climbed out of his truck and went around to help Holly out, just as he'd helped her climb in.

"Thank you."

"You're welcome." He closed her door and opened the back passenger door. "Hank, you wait here with Blaze, where it's nice and warm, okay? I'll be right where you can see me."

"I'll be okay, Daddy. Blaze is gonna take care of me."

Still, Ash hesitated. He'd never left his son alone in the truck before, but the keys were in his pocket, and he could see Hank, and Hank could see him.

"If you want, you can wait in the truck with him," Holly said. "I can talk to the tow driver."

Her simple alternative threw Ash. He'd expected her to sit on the sidelines while he spoke to Junior about towing her SUV back onto the road. He glanced again at Hank, who was engaged in a conversation with Blaze about Willy Whale and Sammy Shark. That helped him make up his mind. He closed the door and took Holly's elbow to escort her over to the tow truck.

Mac's Auto Repair and Tow had been around since before Mac Junior had been born. He introduced Junior to Holly, who shook the hand Junior offered, even though it was obvious he'd been working on someone's engine before driving out to tow Holly's SUV out of a ditch.

"Nice to meet you," Holly said. "Sorry to take you away from the repair part of your business."

"Not a problem, Miss Holly." He squinted at her, shook his head, then headed over to her CR-V. "I been telling the County guys they need to keep this road plowed, but all I get back is budget concerns, yada, yada,

yada." He scratched his beard stubble. "I hope you didn't get hurt."

"Only my pride," she admitted a bit ruefully.

Ash recognized right away that she'd won over Junior, who was a hard sell when it came to meeting new people.

Junior circled the vehicle twice, then climbed back up to the road. "Doesn't look like your car is damaged, and it looks brand new. You can count on me to get it out without a scratch, and if doesn't start, I'll tow it down to the shop and give it a look-see."

"Thank you, so much, Junior. I really appreciate that."

"You best climb back in Ash's trunk and keep warm, Miss Holly."

"I'm fine," she assured him. "How does this all work?"

While Junior described what he had to do to pull her SUV back on the road, Holly listened as if his explanation were the most important thing she'd ever heard.

Ash frowned. He hadn't considered she was one of those people who played others, and maybe she wasn't, but it sure seemed like she was playing Junior. The question was, why?

Or maybe, the question was, what the hell was wrong with Ash's thinking?

"You best stand back now, Miss Holly, and let me get this done."

She nodded and stepped back to stand beside Ash. She looked up at him and said, "You called the right man for the job."

"He's the only tow in Christmas Valley, so he'd better be."

She grinned. "I bet Hank would like to watch this up close."

Ash glanced at the truck and could see his son straining to see what was going on. "You may be right. I'll get him."

He returned with Hank but not Blaze. "Blaze needs a

nap," Hank explained. "We pwayed hard this morning and he's tired."

"I'm sure he is. Thank you for being so considerate."

He smiled and reached down to give her a hug.

Holly hugged him back and gave him a quick kiss on the cheek.

"Junior's hooking up the tow to Holly's car," Ash said, determined to break up the mini lovefest.

Holly swung around to watch, but Hank apparently wasn't finished showing her his affection. His son reached over and patted her head like he sometimes did to Ash when he was holding Hank.

Ash didn't now how he felt about that, but if Holly Morgan was going to rent the cottage, he guessed he damned well better get used to it.

Holly's SUV wouldn't start, but Junior quickly determined it was because the lights had run down the battery. "Dang, if I didn't go off and forget my charger cables. You got any in the truck, Ash?"

"I think so," Ash said, but when he looked, the cables weren't there. "I just remembered, I loaned them to Micah and he hasn't returned them yet."

Junior shook his head chuckling. "Micah's got his mind on the new baby these days."

Ash also shook his head. "A toddler and a baby would be a handful, that's for sure."

Holly listened with interest as they discussed someone she'd never met. Neither man made an effort to fill her in, either.

"Miss Holly, you can ride into town with me and I'll get your CR-V going right quick."

"Thank you." She cast a glance at Ash's truck. Somehow, Blaze had gotten into the front seat and had his front paws on the dash, watching them. Of course, the puppy was smiling.

"Don't worry about Blaze," Ash said. "I don't mind taking him back to the house, but I need to make a stop first to pick up my jumper cables from Micah."

"If you're sure."

"I am."

Satisfied her puppy would be in good hands, she said, "I need to stop and get some groceries on the way home. Where do you recommend I shop?"

Ash gave her directions to the two grocery stores he used. "There's also a RiteAid in the same shopping center as the Grocery Mart."

"And McDonowd's," Hank said. "Me and Daddy wuv McDonowd's."

Holly grinned. "I bet you do." She walked back to the truck and opened the cab door. Blaze leaped into her arms. "You're a naughty boy. You belong in the back seat and I expect you to stay there with Hank."

Blaze puppy *yipped* and licked her.

"He wicks me awa time," Hank said, as if it were a badge of achievement.

"That's because he likes you and you taste good," Holly said.

Hank's dark eyes widened. "I taste good?"

"You must," Holly said, "or he wouldn't lick you."

"Did you hear that, Daddy? I taste good!"

"You sure do," Ash agreed. "Back into your seat you go."

While Ash strapped his son into his carseat, Holly decided to go for broke. "Would you and Hank like to come for dinner tonight?"

Ash froze.

"That is, if you're not busy."

"We're not." He straightened, gave Hank a cheek rub with the back of his knuckle, then closed the door and turned to her. "What time?"

"You tell me. I'll work around your schedule, since I'm assuming Hank is usually in bed around seven."

"Usually. Last night was an exception."

"I gathered," she said, unable to tear her gaze from his. What was she doing? Or, better yet, *why* was she doing it?

"How about five-thirty?"

"Perfect, but don't expect anything extravagant."

His eyes trailed down to her lips, then when he realized he was staring at her mouth, he jerked his gaze back up. "No European cuisine, huh?"

She knew he was teasing, but it gave her an uneasy feeling that he might have figured out who she was. "You'll have to wait and see," she shot back. She blew Hank a kiss and went to join Junior in the tow truck.

Chapter 7

Old Mother Hubbard had nothing on Holly, who spent almost three hundred dollars at the grocery store. It took two carts to haul her purchases to the CR-V, because she literally had to buy everything. The back end of the SUV was crammed full, as was half the back seat.

She headed back to the cottage, happier than she'd been in a long time. When she arrived, Ash's truck was gone. She presumed he was either still at Micah's or doing something else with Hank. Either way, she had plenty of time to carry her purchases inside and put them away before she baked one of the brownie mixes. Chocolate and spaghetti were made to go together.

Around three-thirty, she heard a knock at her door. Being a city girl, the door was locked, and since it didn't have a peephole, she glanced out the window to see who was there. She didn't see anyone, but the knock came again. She lowered her gaze. Hank.

Smiling, she opened the door, kneeling down so she was more his height. "Hi, Hank."

"Hi, Holly. Wanna make some snow angews?"

Holly had shopped at the outdoor store before she hit the grocery store, so she was ready for her first snow adventure. "You bet. I've never made a snow angel, so you'll have to show me how it's done."

He gaped at her with wide eyes. "Never?"

"Nope."

He ran out into the yard, fell backward, and proceeded to move his arms and legs up-and-down. When he finished, he jumped up and ran back to her. "That's how you do it. Hurry up and get your coat on!"

Holly glanced at her watch. She had a little time to play before she finished her dinner preparations. "Be right back."

She grabbed her coat, knit cap, and gloves, then stopped to slip into her new snow boots before she pulled on everything else. Minutes later, she joined Hank in the yard.

Again, he showed her how it was done. Since he was considerably shorter than she was, the fall backward probably didn't seem far to him. As for Holly, she had reservations.

"Are you scared?" he asked.

Surprised by the concern in his voice, she answered honestly. "A little."

"Just cwose your eyes and faw backward."

Following his advice, she did exactly that, adding a little prayer that the snow would pad her head and the big egg on the back of it. To her amazement, it was a fairly soft landing. She laughed and moved her arms and legs as Hank had done.

A shadow crept over her. "You really think you should be falling backward when you have a head injury?"

"Don't be mad, Daddy. Me and Holly just want to make some snow angews."

"I'm not mad, buddy, I'm worried. Holly hit her head

twice yesterday, and she has a big lump on the back of her head."

Hank's face screwed up in distress and then he began to cry. He hurled his little body in her direction, landing on top of her. "I'm sorry, Holly. I didn't mean to hurt you."

"You didn't, sweetie. I'm fine." She thought the reassurance would quell Hank's tears, but if anything, he sobbed harder.

"My son takes things seriously."

"So I gathered," she said, wrapping her arms around him. "It's okay, baby. Cry if you want to. Sometimes I feel like crying, too."

He lifted his head. "You do?"

She nodded. "Crying is good for you. It's helps cleanse the soul."

"What's a sowa?"

"It's the part of us that lives deep inside our body. It's our conscience, our moral values, our love, our anger, our frustrations…." She trailed off, unable to think of anything else on short notice.

"Awo that wivs inside us? Are you sure?"

Above her, Ash crossed his arms over his wide chest and smirked. "I'm as anxious to hear the answer to that as Hank is."

Undaunted, Holly pressed on. "Do you know who God is?"

"Yeah. I pray to Him at bedtime."

"Well, God puts a soul inside every single person. The soul is invisible, like love and anger and frustrations."

Hank's tears seemed to be drying up as the esoteric conversation continued. "When Daddy gets mad, I can see it, and when he says he wuvs me, he gives me a hug and I can feeo that."

Holly glanced at Ash, who stared at her with such intensity, it made her shiver. "All emotions are invisible, because you can't see inside a person to witness them, *but*" —she took a breath, hoping she said the right thing— "when someone is angry and yells or makes a bad face, those are the symptoms of the anger. It's like when you get a cold, you feel horrible inside, but on the outside, you cough and sneeze."

Hank nodded. "I don't like cowds."

"Me, either." She gave him a squeeze, then wiped away his tears. "Ready to get up?"

He nodded. "I'm glad I got a sowa."

The next thing he knew, Ash had him around the middle. Hank squealed as his dad held him with one arm, perpendicular to his big body, and extended a hand to Holly.

She didn't think twice about accepting it.

"Nice job of explaining."

"I think it's more that Hank has a fine mind and he grasped my poor attempt to dig myself out of the hole I dug for myself."

Ash laughed.

"Daddy, put me up on your showders!" Hank begged.

His father said, "Next time. Right now, you and I need to have a talk about you leaving the house without telling me."

"I did tew you," Hank said, now on his feet and eye-to-eye with his father who was on his knees in the snow.

"I don't think so."

Hank nodded vehemently. "Did so. I said, 'Going to Holly's.'"

"Did I hear you?"

"I think so."

"Did I respond that it was okay?"

"Uh, no." Hank's bottom lip began to quiver.

"Next time, find me and make sure I know where you're going."

"Okay. But you found me, didn't you?"

Ash's jaw flexed in frustration.

Holly knew nothing about kids or what to say to them, but she felt compelled to step in. "I think what your dad is saying, Hank, is that anytime you want to come see me, tell him to his face, so he doesn't worry when he can't find you."

Hank looked back at his father. "Were you worried 'bout me?"

"Yes, I was."

"I'm sorry, Daddy. I didn't mean to make you worry." Hank threw his arms around Ash's neck and began to cry again.

"It's okay, son. Just don't do it again, all right?"

Hank nodded, but kept his head plastered against his father's neck.

Ash stood. "What if you and I lie down for a short nap?"

"Okay."

That's when Holly got it that Hank might be overly emotional because he hadn't gotten enough sleep the night before, and that was on her.

"See you at five-thirty." Ash gave her a look devoid of expression and picked up his son, who reached for her.

"Are we having sketti for dinner?" he asked, hugging her.

"We sure are. Hope you're hungry."

"I am!" Unexpectedly, he kissed her cheek. "I wuv you, Holly."

"I love you, too, Hank." Even as she said the words, she knew they were true, even though she didn't know how it was possible to fall in love with a not-quite four-year-old overnight.

Well, really, she did, but the time to think about that was in the middle of the night, when the world was dark and her thoughts and dreams traveled down an even darker path.

Ash needed a cold shower, but he couldn't take one if he had to lay down with his son. For the first time since Hank had been born, he prayed his boy would nod off quickly.

What the hell was wrong with him? He'd never had this kind of a physical reaction before to a woman he'd just met. Yeah, it was true he hadn't been with anyone since Alicia's death, but the way his body had responded, you'd think he was a horny teenager.

As it turned out, Hank fell asleep quickly. Ash covered him with a lightweight throw and left his son's bedroom. He went to his own room and stared out the window at the cottage. What was it about Holly Morgan that grabbed him and wouldn't let go?

Angry that he was dwelling on it, he turned away from the window and went back to his home office, where he had plenty to keep him busy.

The problem was, an hour later, when Hank wandered in from his nap, he hadn't accomplished a damned thing except think about Holly and what it would be like to invite her into his bed.

Rufus and Dinah

Rufus clapped his hands in glee. "Things are moving along swimmingly."

"Not in my opinion," Dinah snapped.

"How is it that you're now on the opposite side of the track from where you normally are, Dinah?"

"How long have they known each other, Rufus? Just over twenty-four hours. How do they even know they like each other?"

"Oh, they know, all right. You don't have attraction like the two of them have without liking each other."

"Who died overnight and made you the Seer of Guardian Angels?"

Startled by her anger, Rufus stared at her, astounded. "What's got you all riled up?"

"You. And them. And that little boy. He loves her already. He's starved for a mother, and Holly fits the bill."

He glanced in the direction of Hank's bedroom. "How do you know that?"

"I'm not really sure, but I do. He formed an instant attachment to Holly and Blaze. If you were really paying attention, you'd notice that both their names have an L in them and Hank says them perfectly, not substituting a W, like he usually does. Even Ash has noticed it."

"By Jove, you're right! You don't think Ash is attracted to Holly just because Hank likes her, do you?"

"No, it's more complicated than that. Ash is a real man and real men have wants and desires, especially if there's a pretty woman in the vicinity. Alicia hurt him deeply, but it's been three years since her death. He's not the type of man to live alone for the rest of his life and he's attracted to Holly. My goodness, did you see the way he looked at her lips? I'd give my eye teeth to have a man look at my lips like that."

"But…you're an angel, Dinah. You can't kiss a man."

"Tell me something I don't know!" she railed.

Rufus stared at her dumbfounded. A moment later, he got an inkling of what was going on with her, or at least, he thought he did.

On second thought, his first thought was ridiculous.

Wasn't it?

Chapter 8

Hank ran ahead of Ash on the pathway leading to the cottage. He pounded on Holly's door with eager anticipation.

Ash halted midway down the path, his heart full of emotion for his son, and for the sight of the cottage, lit up with soft golden light from the inside. From where he stood, it looked warm, inviting, and welcoming…or maybe it was the person inside who projected those things.

Not until Holly had anyone occupied the cottage. Lily had spent two months over the summer helping him clean and update the place. The backyard was large and the kids had taken advantage of that while the two grownups worked. They played and ran through the sprinkler, and had picnics under the shade tree, then napped on blankets under the same tree.

Lily's husband, Sean, joined them to help move the heavy stuff around. Micah and Sylvie showed up to help, too, though Sylvie was pregnant at the time with their second child. They put her in charge of watching the kids and offering helpful decorating suggestions.

Even after all that, the cottage had sat vacant because Ash didn't know if he could handle anyone living so close to him. He'd placed the ad two days earlier, and yesterday was the first day it had run. Not a single person had called or expressed an interest until Holly had knocked on his door.

Talk about Fate. Ash knew she was meant to live there. The question was, how was he going to deal with her being so close?

His friends sometimes offered to "hook him up." In response, he gave them a smile and said he had a business to run and a kid to take care of. To add dating to the mix was a no-go.

But the fact was, sometimes he got lonely for someone to talk to, to share his dreams with, and, if he were being completely honest with himself, his bed. Usually, the loneliness passed in a day or two, but Ash had a strong feeling that whatever there was between him and Holly wasn't going away anytime soon and, lonely or not, that scared the hell out of him.

"Are you coming in?" the woman in question called from the cottage.

"Hurry up, Daddy! I'm starving."

Ash shook his head, like that would actually clear it, and said, "Sorry, I was thinking about work." *Liar!* his conscience screamed back.

He started to take off his boots at the door, but Holly said, "You never have to take off your shoes in my home."

The way she said *home* made him wonder if she planned to live in the cottage forever. How would he survive that? "I see you've got yourself settled in." The minutes the words left his mouth, he wanted to recall the slightly snide tone in which he'd uttered them.

Still, she smiled at him and reached for the jacket he shrugged off. "I bought some winter clothes this morning, then hit the grocery store, and after that, I made some snow angels with my new BFF."

"What's a BFF?" Hank asked, giggling when she tickled him.

"Best friend forever."

"Did you hear that, Daddy? I'm Holly's best friend forever. Wet's eat!"

Holly laughed.

The sound of it curled Ash's toes. If her laughter did that to him, what the hell would happen if they *did* make love and she moaned in pleasure while he adored her body?

The crotch of his jeans got tighter just thinking about it. "Everything smells delicious." He glanced at the table, stunned when he noticed how beautifully it was set. "You didn't have to go all out for us."

She smiled. "I used what I found in the cupboards, with the exception of the mums, which I bought at the grocery store."

"What are we having 'sides sketti?" Hank asked. "And where do I sit?"

"How about between me and your dad," Holly said. "I thought it might make it easier for you to eat at the table if you sat on the dictionary I found in the library."

Hank giggled. "A dictionary! I can get smarter whio I eat."

"I don't know how much smarter you need to be," Holly commented before Ash could say anything.

His father tacked on, "You're already pretty darned smart, buddy."

Hank nodded, as if he knew that, and climbed up into his chair. "Wook, Daddy. Holly made meatbaws."

"So I see," Ash said, waiting for Holly to sit before he did. She'd also made a salad tossed with vinegar-and-oil dressing. The two small vases of mums flanked a big bowl of spaghetti. "Did you make the bread, too?" he asked, surprised that even that came out a bit testy.

She glanced at him with uncertainty. "No. It's a heat-and-serve pugliese. I thought it would go well with the sketti."

He smirked at her response.

She pushed away from the table and stood. "I forgot to ask what you'd like to drink, Hank. I have milk or water."

"Miok, pwease."

She nodded. "Red wine or beer, Ash?"

"What are you having?"

"Wine. It's a Montepulciano."

"That's fine with me."

"Go ahead and serve yourselves. It'll only take me a minute to grab the wine and Hank's milk."

Holly turned away from the table hoping they didn't notice her distress. Why had she invited them? Why was Ash being such a jerk? When would she learn that being alone was the only way to save yourself from heartache?

She grabbed a narrow glass from the cupboard and filled it three-quarters full with milk for Hank. The wine glasses were already on the table, and she'd uncorked the wine earlier. When she reached for the bottle, Ash's big hand settled over hers.

"I'm sorry I was such a dick. I didn't mean to be."

She longed to turn in his arms and tell him it was okay, but it wasn't. "At least you recognize that you were."

He gave a short bark of laughter, then his hand traveled up her arm, forcing her to turn around. "I know this is going to sound stupid, but there's something going on between us." When she didn't respond, he went on. "My reaction to whatever it is was uncalled for and I apologize."

She forced her gaze up to meet his. What she saw in those dark eyes of his started a fire inside her, rendering her silent.

"Don't get mad," he said, "but I have to do this." He lowered his head and kissed her.

Get mad? Was he crazy? She'd been thinking about what it would be like to kiss him all day.

His lips were tentative, then exploratory, and finally, his tongue sought entrance to her mouth.

Holly was fine with kissing him back, but his tongue dueling with hers wasn't on the menu. At least, not yet.

He pulled away and stared down at her, his gaze more heated than ever. "Damn you, Holly."

"What did I do now?" she whispered back, shocked because his words were at complete odds with what his mouth had to say.

"Nothing. And everything." This time, he slid his arms around her and pulled her hard against his body before he took her lips again.

She melted against him and lifted her arms to circle his neck. Her mouth opened of its own volition and she found herself responding in kind to his probing tongue. She was also aware that he was fully aroused.

"Are you gonna eat or keep kissing?" Hank asked.

They jerked apart, surprised to find the boy standing beside them, watching with interest.

"Eat," Ash responded in shaky voice. He grabbed the wine bottle and the glass of milk and headed to the table.

Hank reached for Holly's hand and tugged her along beside him. "Macey says kissing means you wike each other. Do you and Daddy wike each other?" He climbed back up in his chair, waiting for her response.

Holly locked gazes with Ash. "We're still figuring that out."

Hank smiled, as if her answer pleased him. "Can I have more sketti? It's reawy, reawy good."

At two a.m., Holly crawled out of bed and prowled the cottage. How was she supposed to sleep, when all she could think about was kissing Ash Hammell? Did he have to have such tantalizing lips? Did he have to be so good-looking, or so well-built? God knows, she wasn't a superficial person, so she didn't know why she cared, but one thing she did know was that it was the overall package that appealed to her, including his damned brain and his little boy.

At three a.m., she ended up in the art room. She turned on the light at the table and sat down. A moment later, she opened her new sketchbook and began to draw.

At six o'clock, she heard a knock at the door. When she looked out the window, she discovered Ash standing there without his coat on. What he did for a pair of jeans and a sweatshirt should be illegal.

She opened the door about six inches, because she was still in her pajamas. "Good morning."

"Good morning. I would've called, but I don't know your phone number."

She nodded, unable to speak.

"Hank and I wondered if you'd like to come up and have oatmeal with us."

"That sounds delicious. Is Hank up already?"

"No, we discussed it last night, but since your lights have been on, I took a chance you were awake."

"I couldn't sleep."

"Me, either." He stared at her, his eyes holding back nothing. "I can't get that kiss out of my head, Holly. I need another one, and I need it badly."

Her first reaction was to resist letting him know she

felt the same way, but what kind of choice was that? She stepped back, pulling the door all the way open.

Ash entered, kicked it closed with his booted foot, and pulled her into his arms. "You feel so good."

"So do you," she admitted with some reluctance.

He slid his hands beneath her pajama top, scorching her back, and lifted her.

When his mouth closed over hers, Holly thought she'd died and gone to heaven. The kiss went on forever, which was exactly as she'd pictured it in her mind in all the long hours since he'd kissed her the first time.

Finally, he pulled away and stared down at her. "What are we going to do about this?"

"I have no idea. This has never happened to me before."

"Me, either."

She made a sound of disbelief in her throat.

"I'm serious," he said, then blew out a long sigh. "Look, nothing I had with Alicia was anything like what I'm feeling with you."

"Is Alicia Hank's mom?"

He nodded.

"He told me she died on Mount Beady." If she'd been looking for a way to cool his ardor, she'd found it.

Ash's expression grew grim. "I'd better get back to the house, in case Hank wakes up. He'll wonder where I am."

Holly doubted it, but since Ash apparently didn't want to discuss his dead wife, who was she to keep him there kissing her?

Chapter 9

Holly chose dried cherries, sugar, and cream for her oatmeal, and as an afterthought, sprinkled in some chopped nuts. "This is delicious," she said, licking her spoon.

"Glad you like it," Ash said, his eyes on her tongue licking the spoon.

"I had no idea oatmeal could be so good."

"Don't tell me this is the first time you've ever had it."

She hesitated, feeling a little foolish for what her answer had to be. "Actually, it is."

"Where've you been?" he asked in a teasing tone. "Siberia?"

Holly froze. She knew her reaction hadn't gone unnoticed by her host, but she wasn't ready to offer up explanations about her former life. "Nope," she quipped, "but it's so cold there, oatmeal is probably a mainstay."

Ash's eyes narrowed on her in contemplation.

"Wanna make a snowman with me after breakfast?"

Hank asked, oblivious to the back-and-forth between the two adults.

"I'd love to," Holly said, "but you'll have to show me how. I've never built a snowman before."

The little boy's mouth dropped open in surprise. "Never?"

"Nope."

"That's sad," he said with all seriousness.

"It certainly is, but I'm ready to learn."

Hank flashed her a smile. "Daddy makes reawy good bwewberry muffins."

"Does he?" Holly asked, her eyes back on Ash.

"Yep."

"I'd love to taste them sometime." What the heck blueberry muffins had to do with building snowmen, she had no idea.

"Daddy, can we have bwewberry muffins tomorrow?"

"If we have any frozen blueberries left," Ash said.

Satisfied, Hank went back to eating his oatmeal, to which he'd added cranberries, butter, and two teaspoons of sugar. Ash had poured the cream on for him.

"Have you never been in snow country before?"

"Of course, but I was never been allowed to play in it."

"How did that happen?"

"It just did," she said, hoping he wouldn't pursue it further. His eyes lowered to study her lips, which made her body heat up like crazy. "Are you going to help us build a snowman?"

"No. I have paperwork to get done. I'm sure the two of you will do fine without me."

Holly wasn't so sure about that, but she couldn't very well beg him to play in the snow with them. "I'm making hamburgers for dinner. Can you and Hank join me?"

Ash tore his gaze away from her and asked his son, "What do you say, Hank?"

"Hamburgers? Yay! Do you got any brownies weft?"

"Sure do, and some ice cream, too. What do you like on your burger?"

"Mayo and dio pickows."

"Sounds yummy," Holly said. "Maybe I'll try mine that way, too." She glanced back at Ash. His heated gaze left her wondering how she'd survive until he decided to kiss her again.

Ash's stomach growled around one o'clock, reminding him that noon had passed without him fixing lunch for Hank and himself. How had he become so engrossed in work that he forgot about his kid? He headed for the back door, intent on making his way to the cottage. He came to a standstill on the patio, staring in awe at the yard. An army of snowmen in various sizes dotted the landscape.

Hank and Holly had been busy.

Even so, he didn't see them anywhere in the back, which made him wonder if they'd moved their operation to the front, since they'd pretty much used up all the snow between the house and the cottage.

He turned and went back the way he'd come, headed for the front door. Once more, he pulled up short. The front yard was decorated with snow angels, both in pint-size and adult-size versions, with the occasional snow-man thrown in for good measure.

One of the snowmen had wings. Ash stared at it, trying to figure out how they'd attached those wings. Snow-on-snow maybe? But still no Hank and Holly.

Back through the house he went and out the patio door, taking the pathway to the cottage. As he neared, the aroma of cookies baking hit him. He knocked on the door and moments later, Holly pulled it open.

Her little helper, a dishtowel wrapped around him from the waist down, peeked around her, grinning. "Hi, Daddy. We're making cookies."

Ash grinned. "So I gathered. What kind?"

"Oatmeo–raisin and chocowate chip with wawnuts and they're rewwy yummy."

Holly glanced down at his son with a smile and ruffled his hair. "Want to try that again?"

Hank smiled up at her and nodded. "Oatmeal–raisin," he said slowly, obviously concentrating on what he was saying, "and chocolate chip with walnuts. And they're really yummy."

Stunned, Ash leaned down, more or less facing his son at eye level. "That's great, buddy."

Hank nodded, grinning. "Holly said if I can say Holly and Blaze, I can say the letter L in other words, too."

"I guess she was right." He glanced up at her, wondering if his expression reflected his astonishment.

"I hope I didn't overstep," Holly said, clasping her hands behind her.

"You didn't." He flexed his jaw and straightened. "I've tried to work with him, but Lily said it comes with time, and not to push it." He shrugged and added one final thought. "I guess the time arrived with you."

She chewed on her bottom lip, probably thinking that over. "Would you like to discuss it over cookies and milk?"

"I'd prefer coffee instead of milk."

She smiled at him and looked down at Hank. "Good thing we didn't eat all the cookies."

Hank nodding, giggling. "Good thing."

Holly headed back to the kitchen with Hank.

Ash pushed the door closed and followed them.

She could feel his eyes boring into her backside and she wished she'd changed into a baggier pair of jeans after she and Hank played in the snow. On second thought, she realized she probably didn't have any jeans that were baggy, especially after all the cookies she'd eaten.

"It smells like Grandma's kitchen in here," Ash said.

"'Cept Grammy doesn't bake anymore," Hank said.

"That's true, she doesn't."

"Why not?" Holly asked.

"She had a stroke over the summer and after she recovered, she said she lost her zest for cooking."

"More likely, she was tired of cooking. When I'm your mother's age, I expect to be, too."

Ash shook his head, looking a little nonplussed.

"Does she live here?"

"Yeah, she sold her house and moved into one of those all-inclusive senior living places near downtown."

"Does she like it?"

"I think so."

"She has a boyfriend," Hank confided.

"Is that right?" Holly asked, trying not to grin.

"He used to be a fire chief," Hank went on. "Grammy says he's hot."

Holly laughed, but a glance at Ash told her he might not be all that enamored with his mother's new flame (pardon the pun). "I hope I get to meet your grammy."

"She has dinner with us every Wednesday night," Ash said, because Hank was busy licking a wooden spoon. "You're welcome to join us."

"Thank you. I'd like that." She dropped her gaze for fear of her eyes informing him she'd like a lot more than that from him. "Speaking of food, we were just getting ready to make peanut butter and jelly sandwiches for lunch. Care to join us?"

"Sounds good." Ash perused the kitchen with what she could only describe as an eagle eye. "I was going to offer to make them while you clean up your cookie mess, but I see you've already taken care of it."

"I like to clean as I go," Holly said. "Disarray in the kitchen invites bad results."

"That's my theory, too."

"I noticed."

They stared at each other with heated gazes.

Holly blinked first. "Hank's jeans are in the dryer, if you want to get him cleaned up before we eat."

"Ah, do I have to, Holly?" Hank asked. "I wike...I mean, I like my apron."

"And it looks cute on you, but we're done making cookies, aren't we?"

"Yeah, but we're not done baking them." He finished with an angelic smile for good measure.

"Tell you what," Holly said. "If you let your dad get you back into your jeans and get your hands washed, I'll let you take the cookies off the next tray that comes out of the oven."

His big, dark eyes widened. "You will?"

"Yep."

"Hurry up, Daddy. The timer only has three minutes left."

Ash grinned and followed his son to the laundry room, where he pulled two pairs of jeans from the dryer. He folded Holly's and left them on top of the machine, then undid the knot on the dishtowel and helped Hank into his jeans. A small step stool already stood in front of the sink, which told him Hank had washed his hands there earlier.

Holly Morgan was always one step ahead of him, it seemed, and he didn't quite know what to make of that. What was she trying to do, impress him by hanging out with Hank? That didn't feel right, but he knew from past experience, you could never be sure what was going on in a woman's mind.

Hank dried his hands, then ran back to the kitchen. He stood by the counter, bouncing from foot-to-foot, waiting for the cookies to cool enough to be taken off the cookie sheet.

Holly retrieved the step stool from the laundry room and placed it so he could climb up on it. "Remember how I did it?"

He nodded, his expression determined.

"Go slow and you'll do fine," she said. "I'll hold the cookie sheet with the potholder so it doesn't move around on you."

Hank glanced over at his father, as if looking for reassurance.

Ash nodded with a smile. "You can do it, buddy."

Hank turned back to the cookie sheet and began to lift the cookies with the small spatula until all fifteen were transferred to the cooling rack.

"Excellent!" Holly said, hugging him. "You're the best kitchen helper ever."

"I am?" Hank asked.

"Absolutely." She reclaimed the spatula and took it and the cookie sheet to the sink. "Go ahead and sit at the table. Lunch is ready."

It was a simple meal—PB-and-Js, Cheetos, and milk, with cookies for dessert—but it was the best lunch Ash had ever had.

After he took Hank back up to the main house, he finally admitted why. It was the people at the table who had made the food taste so good. It was almost like the three of them were family.

For the first time since he'd learned Alicia had taken a lover, he realized he was thinking about his future, and Hank's, in an entirely new light.

That excited him, but for some reason, it also scared the crap out of him.

Rufus and Dinah

Dinah sighed. "Aren't they just the sweetest couple?"

"I'm worried about Ash," Rufus said. "He's resisting what's ahead of him. I need to consult with someone Upstairs."

"You're supposed to consult with me, Rufus. You and I are working on this assignment together, remember?"

"Not likely I'd forget, but since when do you know everything there is to know about a man who's resisting his fate?"

"I'm not sure he's actually resisting his fate. I think it's more like he's trying to resist trusting a woman again. There's a difference."

"Difference, schmiference."

"Sometimes, I swear, you can be so obtuse."

Rufus put his arms akimbo. "And you can be so insensitive."

"I am not!"

"Are, too!"

"You do realize that you sound like a child right now."

Rufus blinked, but didn't concede. "Ash had a cheating wife and he didn't even know it until she died. That left him with unresolved trust issues."

"To coin a word you love to bandy about, malarkey!"

They glared at each other for several agonizing seconds.

A roar of thunder sounded from overhead.

They ignored it.

Rufus took a step closer to Dinah.

Dinah backed up. "What do you think you're doing?"

"I'm going to kiss you, so you'll know how Ash is feeling."

"I doubt that! If anything, I'll empathize with Holly."

Without considering his actions further, or what the aftermath might be, Rufus closed the distance between them and claimed Dinah's mouth.

To her credit, she didn't bite his lips. Or his tongue.

To his credit, he pulled away after a minute, even though he really didn't want to.

After that, they stared at each other in stunned silence.

Chapter 10

Holly started. "Was that thunder?"

"I don't see how it could be, since it's winter." Ash went to the window and looked out at the sky. "Nothing but stars and more stars. Still, this has been a weird year for weather and stranger things have happened in the valley."

"Like what?" Holly asked. Genuinely curious, she joined him at the window. He looked down at her and she knew what was coming next.

"At the moment, I can't think of any examples." He inched around to face her and lowered his head, touching his lips to hers ever so gently. He whispered, "All I can think about is you. Open your mouth for me, Holly."

She complied and the next thing she knew, she was snug against his body. She curled her arms around his neck, silently begging for more.

"Daddy, does it feel good to kiss Holly like that?" Hank asked, as if he were Ash's common sense on short legs.

Ash pulled away and stared down into her eyes. "Yes."

"Do you like it, too, Holly?"

With a jerky nod of her head, Holly said, "Yes."

"I'm glad." He turned and walked back to the TV to finish watching *Toy Story*, a DVD his dad had brought along.

Now Holly knew why. "The burgers are almost ready."

"I'm ready, too."

"So I noticed. Come help me in the kitchen."

A slight smiled flitted across his dirty-dog-handsome face. "I'll be in the kitchen," he told Hank, who may or may not have heard him, since he was once again engrossed in the movie.

Once they reached the kitchen, Ash glanced around. "The table is set, the condiments are on it, and there's a bowl of chips and a fruit salad also on the table. What do you need my help with?"

"As if you didn't know."

He grinned and took her in his arms again.

It felt so right for him to kiss her and for her to kiss him back. Holly would have been happy to keep at it all night long, but she was also starting to crave more than kisses. She wanted to go skin-to-skin with him, damn the consequences.

The memory of another time she'd done that hit her with the force of hurricane winds. That person was so *not* the Holly she was today. She pulled away with reluctance and backed up a few steps.

"What's wrong?"

How could she answer that? *I had a thought about damning the consequences, when I know good and well how doing so can change my life irrevocably, and not in a good way.* Or maybe, *I can't because for some inexplicable reason, I'm falling in love with you, and that's simply not possible.*

In the end, she said nothing, and instead moved toward

the stove. She flipped the hamburger patties, lowered the heat, then stood debating what to do that didn't involve kissing.

Ash took the decision out of her hands when he pulled her back into his arms. A short time later, he released her. "The movie's almost over."

"Is it?"

He nodded. "And I'm sure the hamburger patties are probably done."

"I'm sure you're right." With a sigh, she reclaimed her arms and turned back to the stove, shutting off the burner.

Ash came up behind her and slid his arms around her waist. "Lily invited Hank for a sleepover on Friday night. I said yes."

Friday night. That was only five nights away. "That should be fun for Hank."

"It can be fun for us, too."

She turned to face him. "Are you asking me on a date?"

"I guess I am. I'll cook you dinner and afterward, we'll have our own sleepover."

He couldn't have made his intentions any clearer, but that memory she'd rather not dwell on reminded her that having sex with a man she'd only known for two days— or seven by Friday—could result in a perilous journey. "Can I let you know tomorrow?"

He frowned, but said, "Sure." After a moment's hesitation, he said, "I didn't mean to rush you."

Should she explain herself, or did she even owe him an explanation? "It's not that, but as I mentioned previously, I've never felt like this before. I have to think about it."

"We're kind of in the same boat."

His admission didn't make her feel any better. She even wondered if he'd said it just to convince her to crawl into bed with him. No, he wouldn't do that. He wasn't that kind of man. At least, she didn't think he was. Or maybe she was kidding herself because of how her mind, her heart, and her body were reacting to him. "What's your qualifier?"

By his expression, he knew what she was asking, but he was agonizing over his response. "I met Alicia in a bar while I was on leave. She came on to me, I was horny, we screwed, and Hank was conceived. We got married when she realized she was pregnant and then my SEAL team shipped out. Hank was born while I was in the Middle East. By the time he was seven months old, I'd fulfilled my ten-year commitment, so I came home. A month later, Alicia told me she and her friends were headed to the ski resort at Mount Beady for a book-club weekend. The next day, the cops showed up at my door to tell me she'd been killed in a snowmobile accident with her lover."

"I'm sorry your wife cheated on you, Ash. I've never understood why people don't get divorced first, then start seeing other people." Her own story would take a little longer to tell, which didn't mean she was up to sharing it just then.

He shook his head. "I was crazy about Hank, and I spent more time with him than she did when I got back." He sighed, and went on. "To be completely honest, she and I didn't click sexually, or any other way, which I imagine is why she took up with another man."

Holly's heart broke for him. Her own marriage had been short and terrifying. She knew what it was like not to have that ongoing sexual spark, and what it was like to have a cheating spouse.

"The movie's over, Daddy. Is it time to eat?" When Ash didn't respond, Hank yanked on his jeans. "Is it?"

Ash gave her a gentle peck and dropped his arms. "It sure is, buddy. You want milk or water with your burger?"

"How about a root beer?" Hank suggested instead.

"No soda for you, remember? Not until you're five."

Hank's lower lip went out for a moment, then he grinned. "Maybe orange juice then?"

Ash glanced at Holly, who nodded.

"Orange juice it is, little man." He picked up his son and plopped him down in his chair, then went to get the juice.

Holly put the hamburgers on buns and carried the plate to the table while Ash filled Hank's glass with OJ. Once they were seated, she watched as Ash put mayo and dill pickles on Hank's burger. It was a testament to the type of man he was, that he took such excellent care of his child. "Ash?"

His eyes still on his son's burger, he said, "Yeah?"

"I'd love to spend Friday night with you."

His head jerked up and he smiled, which threw her body into a tizzy. He really ought to smile more often. "Good."

"I'm having a sleepover at Auntie Lily and Uncle Sean's on Friday night," Hank informed her. "I was worried about Daddy being all alone, but now I'm not." He gave her one of his angelic smiles. "I hope you and Daddy have fun together."

Holly refused to make eye contact with Ash when she said, "I'm sure we will."

Chapter 11

The snow started falling overnight, leaving another foot on the ground by morning. When the sun came out, it made the army of snowmen look like they'd been dusted with diamonds.

Just before noon, Ash showed up at Holly's door with Hank in his arms. "I hate to ask this, but my regular babysitter committed to watching some other kids because the schools are closed due to the snow."

Holly smiled at him. "Let me save you some time. If you're asking if I can watch Hank, I'd love to."

"Thanks. I have to go out on a search-and-rescue." He added, "I don't know how long I'll be gone."

"I promise to take good care of him, however long it takes you." She frowned. "Is it going to be…that is…." She trailed off, not wanting to mention the word *dangerous* for fear it might scare Hank.

Apparently, Ash read her mind. "It usually is, but I have a good crew, and Ryker is going to join in, since we need a helicopter to get where we're going."

"Ryker?"

"Ryker Manning. He lives out of town a ways."

"I see," she said, though she really didn't. How much further out of town could he be than Ash was?

"His wife, Jani, is stuck out there because the road hasn't been plowed yet, but she'll check in with you by phone."

"If you had my number," Holly teased.

"You're right. I never did get it."

"Daddy, put me down so I can play with Blaze."

Ash set his son down, and that's when Holly noticed the overnight bag. "You came prepared."

"That's me. Always prepared." His expression expressed his chagrin. "I hope this isn't too much of an imposition."

"It isn't. Get your phone out and I'll give you my number." A minute later, when she was sure Hank was out of earshot, she asked, "How dangerous is it going to be?"

"We never know until we get there. We're after a couple of skiers who ventured off the ski run and got caught in the side slide of a small avalanche."

Holly nodded. "I'll pray for their safe recovery…and your safe return."

"Thank you," he said, and pulled her close for a short but earth-shattering kiss. "Be forewarned, since we're in snow season, I may get called out again while I'm out."

"I understand. Don't worry about Hank. He's in good hands."

"Of that, I have no doubt." He called to his son. "How about a goodbye kiss and hug for your dad?"

Hank let go of Blaze long enough to give his father both, then settled down with the puppy again and proceeded to tell Blaze where his dad was off to.

Holly wasn't quite ready to say goodbye. "Hank, put your coat back on," she said, grabbing hers from the coat hook just inside the door. "We'll walk your dad to the truck."

"Yippee! We can make more snow angels in the front yard."

Holly appreciated his youthful enthusiasm, but at the moment, she was more concerned about Ash. Was he worried about leaving his son with her, possibly for several days, when he really didn't know her from Adam?

Blaze bounded out the door ahead of them, happy to be frolicking in the snow. Hank chased after him, happy as could be.

Ash grabbed Holly's hand. His dwarfed hers, and it gave her a sense of security she'd never felt before.

Neither had gloves on. If he felt the heat of her skin like she felt his, she knew Friday night was going to be something special.

"Most of what's in Hank's overnight bag are his Toy Story toys." Ash dug into his pocket and handed her a key. "This unlocks both the front and back doors, if you need to grab extra clothes for him, or if your power goes out and you want a warm fire, or if—"

"I get it. Is there a pawn shop in town where I can hock all your expensive stuff?"

He looked down at her in shock, then realized she was teasing. "Harry's Seconds. He's an old school friend. Just let him know whose stuff it is, and he'll give you a terrific deal on it."

Holly laughed. "Good to know." She glanced at Ash's truck, which he'd already backed out of the garage. "If you're not back by Wednesday—"

"I should be, unless something else crops up." He pulled open the door of his truck.

"But if you're not, would it be okay if Hank and I go

pick up your mom and bring her home for dinner?"

"Why would you want to do that?"

"You said you have dinner with her every Wednesday, and I'm sure she'd love to see her grandson."

"Well, yeah, but…." He looked off in the distance, then back at her. "Actually, I think she'd like that. Since she had the stroke, she's seems to enjoy a pattern of sameness."

Holly smiled. "Will she want to bring her boyfriend along?"

"Probably, and whether or not you feel up to having both of them is up to you."

"What's his name?"

"Harry Hamilton, Senior. His son owns the pawn shop."

"How does he feel about his dad having a girlfriend?"

"His mom died when he was in high school. He thinks it's about time his dad finally settled down with a good woman again."

"What's your mom's name?"

"Betsy."

"Is your dad dead, or are they divorced?"

"Dad died about five years ago. He and some buddies were hunting, Dad got separated from them, and he wandered around lost so long, he froze to death." He turned grim eyes toward the mountains beyond Christmas Valley. "He's the reason I do search-and-rescue."

"You're an honorable man, Ash."

He grunted and she could tell he was embarrassed by her assessment of him.

"Just to be clear, it's okay for me to take Hank in my car?"

"Yes. Damn, I forgot about his booster seat. Let me grab it." He opened the passenger cab and reached across to unhook the booster. He handed it over to Holly, then leaned down and kissed her. "I'd rather stay here, but…."

"I know, you have lives to save." She forced a smile. "Stay safe. See you when you get back."

He kissed her again, then waved goodbye to Hank, who was rolling in the snow with Blaze. Moments later, he backed out of the drive and within seconds, his red truck was a dot in the distance, then nothing.

"Holly, wanna build a snowman?"

"Absolutely." She set the booster down on the cleared front steps and shoved the house key into the front pocket of her jeans. "Let's limit it to three," she said, smiling as she pulled on her gloves. "That way, we won't use up all the snow."

"How about four?"

"Nope, Three it is."

He shrugged his small shoulders. "How about two now, and two more later?"

Holly laughed. One way or another, Hank Hammell, persistent boy genius, was going to build four snowmen today. Already, he was a lot like his father.

The thought tickled her so much, she asked, "What do you think about dressing the first two we build?"

"Really?"

"Really. Race you to the cottage."

"I thought we were going to make snowmen."

"We are, but we can't dress them in the clothes we're wearing, now can we?"

He grinned up at her. "I guess not! C'mon, Blaze. Race you to the cottage."

Rufus and Dinah

Rufus pondered his current situation. Dinah hadn't uttered a word since he'd kissed her. Why couldn't she be more like Holly and accept it for what it was? Not that he *knew* what it was, but he'd certainly liked it.

Hours went by and he couldn't stand the silence any longer. "When are you going to speak to me again?"

"Maybe never!"

"You're going to have to, Dinah. We're on assignment here, remember? We have to make sure Ash and Holly get together."

"They *are* getting together," she reminded him. "As soon as he gets back from his search-and-rescue operation."

"About that, he's going to get another call tomorrow, after he wraps up the avalanche rescue."

"By all that's holy, I *hate* it when you spring advance information on me!"

"I can't help it."

"Why doesn't the Big Guy ever favor me that way?"

Rufus gritted his guardian angel teeth. Dinah knew he didn't approve of her use of the moniker Big Guy, but no matter how many times he'd asked her not to refer to God that way, she continued to do so. He was beginning to think he understood why. She enjoyed being perverse. "One guardian angel per team is assigned advance information status, as you very well know, and I happen to be the one He chose for this team."

She cast a stormy look in his direction. "That doesn't mean I have to like it."

"But you did like my kiss."

Instead of agreeing with him, she said, "I spent some time reviewing the Angel Book of Rules, and I didn't see anywhere that kissing is permitted."

"It also doesn't say kissing is *not* permitted, does it?"

"How would you like to be knocked off this roof again?"

He barked out a laugh. "I'll be ready for it this time. You won't be able to send me over the edge again. Or at least, not the edge of the roof."

She smirked at him. "That's what you think." She waved her guardian angel arms in his direction.

Startled by her action, Rufus slid down the roof and into the snow bank on the back side of the cottage. "Darn you, Dinah!"

"Serves you right," she called down to him. "While you're down there, think on how we're going to ensure that Ash and Holly end up married before Christmas."

Chapter 12

It snowed so hard on Tuesday, Holly and Hank stayed inside. They spent the day coloring, playing, watching kid videos, and eating their meals in front of the fireplace.

She imagined that whoever had owned the property before had spent most of his or her time in the art room, hence the need for the fireplace.

Hank was intensely interested in watching Holly draw and asked if she could teach him how. She gladly obliged.

While the child's final products weren't polished, he definitely had a knack for it. She promised, if the snow let up the next day, they'd buy a couple of frames and gift one of the pictures to his dad and one to his grandma.

Hank jumped up-and-down. "For Christmas presents?"

Holly hadn't considered giving them as Christmas gifts, but she liked the idea. "Yes! We'll buy some wrapping paper and ribbon, too."

"Yaaayy!"

When it was time to tuck Hank in for the night, he fell asleep before she'd read two pages of the book he'd picked out. Apparently, the trick to wearing out a child was to keep him busy all day long. He'd had fun and Holly loved every minute she spent with him.

It was a win-win all around.

The sun was out by the time they awoke Wednesday morning. Hank ran screaming into her bedroom that the snow was already melting.

Holly doubted that, but she did know, if the sun shined, the snow would melt, eventually. "Let's have breakfast and see how the road is around lunch time. If it looks like we can make it into town, we'll eat at McDonald's before we buy the picture frames, then we'll go pick up your grandma."

"Grammy will be so excited to see us," he cried.

"I'm excited to meet her." Holly threw back the covers. "Will you let Blaze out so he can do his business?"

Hank nodded and scurried off with Blaze racing beside him.

Holly loved Blaze, but if she ever had to leave Christmas Valley for any reason, she'd have to make a huge sacrifice and leave her dog with Hank. It would be difficult for her, but Hank would be devastated if she took Blaze with her. She couldn't do that to him.

Mid-morning, someone knocked on the door. Holly, Hank, and Blaze went to see who it was.

"Micah!" Hank yelled and rushed forward to hug the man around his knees.

Micah squatted down. "How's it going, buddy?"

"Me and Holly are having lots of fun. Are you driving the snow plow today?"

"Sure am." He pushed to his feet and said, "Micah

Barrow." He extended his hand to her. "It's good to meet you, Holly."

"Ash has spoken about you and Sylvie. It's good to meet you, too."

"Just wanted to let you know the road is plowed and I'm going to hit your driveway next, in case you want to go into town."

"Thank you! Hank and I were hoping the roads would be passable, but I completely spaced the driveway." Was it any wonder, when she and Hank had been inside for almost twenty-four hours?

Micah nodded and pulled a business card out of his pocket. "Here's my cell and home numbers, along with Sylvie's number. If you're free this afternoon, she'd like to meet you."

"Goody!" Hank said. "We can see baby Tara and play with Logan. Can we bring Blaze, too?"

"If Holly says it's okay, it's fine by us. He can play with Nugget."

"I take it a Nugget is a dog," Holly noted wryly.

"He's a golden retriever, like Blaze. He was my bomb K-9 when I was in the military. He developed an allergy to poppy plants, so he was discharged, and I was able to adopt him when I discharged."

A bomb K-9? Wow. "That must have been some dangerous work for both of you."

"It was, but fortunately, we both survived."

"Did you and Ash serve together?"

"We were Marines at the same time, and sometimes our paths crossed, but I wasn't interested in being a SEAL, like he was. We also grew up together, though he's two years older than me. Small town, you know?"

Holly didn't, because she'd grown up in the big city, but she was beginning to understand how things worked here. "We'll try to make it over to meet Sylvie today before we pick up Hanks' grandmother. She's joining us for dinner tonight."

"Have you met her yet?"

"No."

Micah grinned. "You're in for a treat. Betsy is a character. Next to Murph's mom, she amazes me more than almost anyone, except for Sylvie, of course."

Holly smiled. "Of course. Who's Murph?"

"Murph O'Donnell. He quarterbacked for the Stallions until he injured his shoulder."

"What's so special about his mother?"

"Livvy's a psychic. Maybe you've heard of her? Her professional name is Olivia Strangewayes."

"I haven't," Holly said, though she thought Strangewayes was a way better pseudonym than Sophisti-Kitty. "But I've only been in town since Saturday."

"She's a friend of Betsy's."

"Maybe we should invite her to join us for dinner. It would make for interesting conversation to have a psychic at the table."

Micah laughed. "You don't know the half of it. I'd better get on that driveway. See you guys later."

He no sooner climbed up into the snowplow than her phone rang.

The caller identified herself as Jani Manning. "I'm sorry I didn't call yesterday," Jani said. "I wasn't feeling well and spent most of the day in bed."

"Are you doing okay now? Micah is clearing my driveway, so I could drive out with some soup or—"

"Thanks for offering, but Ryker got home last night and took me to the doctor first thing this morning. You're among the first to know that what I thought was the flu is actually pregnancy."

"Congratulations!" Holly said, and she meant it.

"Thank you. God has blessed us with a miracle and Ryker and I are both super excited about it."

For the first time, Holly thought seriously about what it would be like to carry a baby she'd made with Ash.

At eleven, Hank said he was hungry. Even though they'd slept in until eight, they'd only had cinnamon toast and milk for breakfast, and Holly realized she was hungry, too. They made sure all the lights were out before they put on their winter gear and entered the garage. She lifted Blaze into the crate in the back area, then got Hank settled in his booster seat.

"I like your car, Holly."

"Thank you. It's likes you, too."

He grinned and gave her a hug.

When they got on the road, Hank asked, "If Daddy has to work on Friday, how will I get to Auntie Lily's house?"

"I'll take you."

"What are we fixing for dinner tonight?"

"I don't know yet. What does your grammy like?"

"Sketti."

"We just had that."

"I know, but she likes it."

And apparently, so did Hank. "What else does she like?"

He thought a moment. "Chicken."

That offered up some possibilities. "After we have lunch, we'll stop by Micah's house, then we'll hit the grocery store, and then we'll pick up your grammy. How does that sound?"

"Good. Grammy likes brownies, too."

"There's still half a pan left," Holly assured him, but her mind was on how she could prepare chicken that Ash's mother would like.

At McDonald's, Hank ate a Happy Meal and Holly had

a Southwest Chicken Salad. Afterward, they spent almost an hour at Sylvie's. Logan and Hank played together and Sylvie let Holly hold Tara and feed her.

"You're a natural," Sylvie said.

"Aren't all women?" Holly asked.

"Not these days."

Holly thought of her own mother and realized Sylvie was right. Still, she was pleased that Sylvie thought she was good at tending a baby. "Do you have any recipes using chicken?"

"I do." Sylvie grabbed a binder holding recipe cards, pulled out several, and went to the home office to scan them.

"Which one do you think Ash's mother would like best?" Holly asked.

"Betsy will like whatever you make, but if you want to wow her, do the chicken breast stuffed with spinach and fontina cheese. You can serve it with rice and maybe cooked carrots and it'll be a good meal."

Next, they hit the frame store and selected two nice mats to fit inside them. At the meat counter inside the grocery store, the butcher also gave her a shortcut recipe for chicken cordon bleu, which sounded good, too. Torn between the options, Holly purchased the ingredients for both recipes and headed off to pick up Betsy Hammell.

"Good thing we called Grammy afore we left."

"Yes, it is," Holly agreed, though it was obvious Betsy had already been given a heads-up. Had Ash been in contact with his mother and told her that Holly had rented the cottage, or had Olivia Strangewayes given her the news?

"Grammy!" Hank cried, running to give his grandmother a hug and a kiss. "Did you miss me?"

"Yes, I did," Betsy assured him. "All the way to the moon and back."

"That's a long way!" he said with wide eyes. "Can

Auntie Livvy have dinner with us?"

His grandmother grinned. "Absolutely. Since your daddy is off rescuing someone else, it'll be just us three girls and you, and we'll spoil you rotten." She looked up and said, "Hello, Holly. Nice to meet you in person."

Holly's head was spinning from the implications of *us three girls*. Belatedly, she remembered that Micah had referred to Olivia Strangewayes as Livvy. It *was* going to be an interesting evening. "Nice to meet you, too, Mrs. Hammell."

Betsy shook her head. "Please, call me Betsy. Mrs. Hammell makes me feel even older than I am."

She certainly didn't look old. "Betsy it is. Ash said you had a stroke recently. How are you doing?"

"I feel like I could run with the reindeer," she said, which made Hank laugh. "In some ways, I'm sorry I sold my house, but then I remember how much work it was to clean, and I'm glad I'm here."

She punctuated that observation with a cheeky grin that reminded Holly of Hank. "Do they offer housekeeping services here?"

"They do, but I prefer to do my own cleaning."

Holly understood that all too well. "I take it Mr. Hamilton won't be joining us for dinner."

Betsy smirked. "Not tonight. Harry and his son are playing poker with the boys."

Holly smiled. She liked poker, as long as it was played for pennies. Her brain tracked back to Livvy. "Are Livvy and Olivia Strangewayes the same person?"

"Yes. Did Ash tell you about her?"

"Actually, Micah did. I've never met a psychic before."

"Then you're in for a treat," Betsy responded rather ambiguously.

Curious though she was, Holly decided to leave the remainder of her dozen questions for later.

Chapter 13

In the end, Holly decided to make the spinach-and-cheese stuffed chicken. Since the wine sauce cooked down, it wouldn't affect Hank and it really sounded delicious. She also made long-grain-and-wild rice and the cooked carrots, as Sylvie had suggested, along with heat-and-serve dinner rolls.

Hank and Blaze played at her feet while she prepared the meal. Betsy and Livvy sat at the bar, sipping wine and snacking on Wheat Thins, cheese, and salami. They must have thought they were unobtrusive with their information gathering, but Holly caught on immediately.

She'd spent years not answering questions about her life, so there wasn't anything they'd get out of her that she didn't want them to know.

"I see you made an extra chicken breast," Betsy said.

"For Ash, in case he comes in late. He might be hungry."

The two older women shared a pleased glance.

Holly caught the exchange and almost told them not to

get their hopes up, but decided against it, especially since she already had *her* hopes up.

"How did you like modeling, Holly?"

In the process of setting the table, Holly froze. How could Livvy possibly know that she modeled? Then she remembered. Livvy was a psychic. Maybe a *real* one. "Not at all," she said lightly. "That's why I'm an illustrator now."

"Do you work freelance," Betsy asked, "or for a company?"

"A publishing company hired me as a freelance artist for their nonfiction division. I like having my independence."

Both the ladies nodded, as if satisfied with her answer.

"Hank, milk or something else to drink with dinner?" Holly asked.

"Root beer," he said without hesitation.

"Nice try," Holly said, grinning. "Milk it is."

He shrugged, as if he'd expected her response.

"Why do you always choose root beer?" Betsy asked him.

Hank set one of his cars in motion.

Blaze chased after it.

"Ignoring me doesn't answer the question, young man."

Hank looked up and flashed her one of his angelic smiles. "Macey let me have a little taste of hers once, and I liked it." He stood and went over to his grandmother. "Don't tell her mom, okay? It was just a tiny sip."

"I won't, but you know how your dad feels about you drinking soda."

He nodded, his expression somber.

"Speaking of dad," Livvy said. "Set one more plate, Holly. Ash is headed home now."

Holly tried to curb her excitement when Ash walked in from the garage.

Hank, on the other hand, screamed, "Daddy!" and ran to his father. She envied his free spirit and longed to do exactly what he'd done.

Ash gave his son a kiss and a hug, then proceeded to do the same to his mother and Livvy. For Holly, he had a warm, "Hi, Holly," but no kiss and no hug.

Her heart stood still and her hopes plummeted. Gone two days and he'd already lost his desire for her.

A moment later, he proved her wrong.

She met his hungry gaze, hoping he understood she felt the same way. He *wanted* to give her a kiss and a hug, but for the moment, she had to be satisfied with a simple greeting. She turned and went to the stove.

"Something smells good," he said, sniffing the air.

"Sylvie gave me a couple recipes to try," Holly said, pulling the carrots off the stove to drain.

"Are you hungry as a bear, Daddy?" Hank asked.

"I'm hungry as two bears tonight, buddy. I haven't eaten since breakfast."

"How come?"

"We had to find a little boy who got lost in the woods."

"Is he okay?" Holly asked, turning a worried glance on Ash. "Did you find him?"

"We did, and he is, though he was colder than a witch's...." He trailed off, knowing the adults in the room got the picture, even though he'd left off *tit*, a word his son didn't need to learn at this juncture in his life. "He was scared, but at least he had sense enough to shelter under a copse of trees."

"Anyone we know?" Betsy asked.

"Someone visiting grandparents out past the Christmas

Valley Inn. His granddad took him out sledding and he wandered away. Since there were five kids, his granddad didn't notice immediately, but lucky for the kid, we got the call right away." He shook his head. "Otherwise, his story could've had a different ending."

"Thank God, it didn't," Holly said. "How old is he?"

"Seven." Ash glanced at Livvy. "Did you get anything on him?"

"No, but then I don't always, especially if it has a happy ending."

He shook his head. "I figured I would've heard from you, if you had." He pulled off his coat and hung it on the hook by the back door. "Man, I'm beat."

"Wash up," Holly said. "Dinner will be on the table by the time you finish."

He stared at her for a moment, then let his gaze wander slowly down her body before it darted left to Hank and Blaze. "C'mon, buddy. You need to wash your hands, too, since you've been playing with Blaze."

Holly hadn't realized she'd been holding her breath, but when he walked away, she released it.

"You and Ash will make beautiful children," Livvy said.

Holly turned to stare at her. "Ash and I don't even know each other yet."

Livvy smiled in return and winked at her.

Betsy put away what was left of the appetizers while her friend filled the water glasses.

After that, dinner went off without a hitch. Ash helped keep the conversation going by relating the successful rescue efforts of his team, from the avalanche to the missing child.

When dinner and dessert were over, and clean-up was complete, everyone moved to the living room. Hank was allowed to stay up a half-hour later than usual, but he started to nod off sooner. He kissed everyone goodnight and Holly offered to get him into his jammies and into bed. By the time she returned to the living room, Ash was sound asleep in his chair.

Holly volunteered to drive the ladies back to their respective residences. Her SUV was still parked part-way up the drive leading to the cottage, making it easily accessible from the back door out of the kitchen.

Holly dropped Livvy off first. When the psychic climbed out, she said, "It was a pleasure to meet you, Holly. You're good for Ash."

Holly knew the heat level between her and Ash, ranked on a scale of one-to-ten, was at least an eleven, but she was stunned by Livvy's comment, nonetheless, especially coupled with her earlier comment about beautiful children.

Livvy smiled and closed the door. Holly waited for her to go inside before she drove way.

"Livvy tends to speak her mind," Betsy said, smiling.

"She's interesting, that's for sure."

Betsy chuckled. "You took it well when she said you're good for Ash. As it happens, I agree with her."

Holly didn't expect to hear that from Ash's mother. Her short-term former mother-in-law had hated her guts. "Because of his wife, you mean?"

"Yes. For a man who took his wedding vows seriously, he was devastated when he discovered Alicia was cheating on him. It's been three years since she died. He's never once dated in all that time."

"He's afraid to take a chance."

Betsy nodded, then leaned over and hugged Holly before she climbed out of the SUV. "See you next Wednesday. Let's have sketti, shall we? Hank loves it and so do I." She headed for the entrance, where a tall, good-looking older gentleman waited for her just inside the double-glass doorway. They hugged, then kissed, and finally, he took her hand and off they went.

Holly shook her head, smiling. Betsy Hammell had a little Cupid in her, fueled, no doubt, by Livvy's assurances that Ash and Holly were meant to be together.

Would she and Ash hit it off to the point of having a permanent relationship, or was whatever it was going on between them destined to be nothing but a quick fling?

Just because Livvy was a psychic, did that really mean she was savvy about such matters?

How would Hank feel about having her as his mother?

Was Ash even interested in getting married again?

The questions kept coming at her, but she had no answers.

Regardless, Holly knew one thing for sure. She could hardly wait for Friday night.

Back at the cottage, she pointed the garage door opener at the door to raise it. She pulled inside and shut off the SUV, which automatically unlocked the doors. A moment later, her door opened unexpectedly.

There stood Ash, in all his masculine glory.

Her insides began to tingle in anticipation. "Where's your coat?" she asked inanely.

"Where I hung it up. You forgot something."

"I know. I was just coming to get him," she said, thinking he meant Blaze.

"You should have woken me to take Mom and Livvy home."

"You were sleeping so soundly, it seemed silly to wake you." In an unconscious gesture, she licked her lips. "Besides, I do know how to drive."

He stared down at her for a moment, then grinned. "I had no idea you were a smart ass."

"I can be," she agreed, unable to hold back a grin of her own. "It's good to have you home again."

"Was Hank too much of a handful?"

"No. He's a dream child."

"I doubt that, but he is a pretty good kid." He studied

her in silence for several moments. "I missed you."

"How can you miss someone you barely know?"

"I have no idea, but I did." He reached across her to undo the seatbelt.

His arm brushed against her breasts, setting her insides on fire. She uttered a soft moan.

"I don't know if I can wait for Friday night, Holly."

"I don't know if I can, either."

He tugged her out of the SUV and into his arms. His kiss was that of a starving man.

She returned it like she was a starving woman.

"Come back to the house for…." He trailed off with a shrug.

"I need to get Blaze."

"He's sound asleep in Hank's room." He kissed her again and sighed. "Will you come to bed with me, Holly?"

"What about Hank?"

"He's not usually an early riser. You could be gone before he gets up."

That was the problem. Holly didn't want to be gone. She wanted to wake up in Ash's arms and stay there all day. "Does he wake up in the middle of the night?"

"No. He's a sound sleeper."

"What about Friday night?"

"Who says we can't have both?"

Not me, she thought and pulled his head down for another kiss.

Rufus and Dinah

"OMG!" Dinah cried. "They're going to *do* it tonight."

"Simmer down, girl. Sex does *not* equal marriage, and that is our assignment goal, remember?"

"How could I forget? You keep reminding me every five minutes."

They watched from the rooftop as Ash grabbed the remote control and shut the garage door behind them as they walked hand-in-hand back to his house.

"What shall we do while they're, you know, *doing* it?" Rufus inquired, his voice husky.

"We do have another couple we could see to," Dinah reminded him, wondering what that husky voice of Rufus's was all about.

"They're doing fine."

"That was this morning. A lot can happen in a few hours."

Rufus looked down at her. "First thing we should do is get off the rooftop." He wagged a finger in her face. "And I don't mean that you should push me off again, then float down to laugh at me when I'm covered in snow."

"I only did that because…." She reared back as he leaned closer. Her guardian angel face flamed red when she realized what he had in mind. "Don't you dare try kissing me again, Rufus!"

He grabbed her hand and in the next instant, they were sitting together on the double swing hanging from the huge maple tree on the other side of the yard.

"I'm warning you, Rufus. I reread the Angel Book of Rules today, and there is no mention of kissing."

"I thought we already had that settled, Dinah." He put his arm over her shoulders and urged her closer. "It's just kissing, isn't it? The Big Guy might release more thunder, but other than that, what's he going to do?"

"Snap a lightning bolt down on us?" Dinah suggested, her eyes on his lips.

Angus got a little excited when she licked her own lips while studying his. He'd watched Holly do that just a while ago, and now he knew how Ash felt. "We're guardian angels, not humans, so I don't believe a lightning bolt would affect us one way or another."

Dinah trembled. Was it because of Rufus or her next thought? "He could always send us downstairs to you-know-where."

"He could." Rufus leaned closer. "But he won't. Aren't you the one who once told me that you'd like to go human?"

She nodded and threw her arms around his neck. "You'd better make it good, Rufus, because this is the last kiss you're getting."

He smirked, then whispered against her lips, "I doubt it."

Chapter 14

Ash opened the patio door and let Holly go in ahead of him. He locked it behind him and tugged her further into the room.

Holly was so excited, she was shaking with anticipation. She barely noticed Blaze, who'd come to greet her.

Ash unbuttoned her coat, then slipped it off her shoulders. It landed on the puppy, who wriggled out from under it and went running back toward Hank's room. Ash took her hand again and led her down the hall, turning off lights as they went.

They stopped at Hank's door. Thanks to the nightlight, they were assured that the boy was asleep. Blaze raised his head and smiled at them, then lowered it again and dozed off.

"Are you sure this is okay?" she asked when they reached his bedroom doorway.

"It is, as long as you're in agreement. I don't want you to do anything you don't feel comfortable doing."

"I could say the same for you."

"I suppose Mom told you I haven't dated since Alicia died."

"She might have mentioned it," Holly said, and decided not to reveal the rest of the conversation, or what Livvy had said.

He smiled down at her. "Something told me to wait for the right woman to come along."

"Do you think that's me?"

"I don't *think* it. I *know* it's you."

"I have baggage."

"We all have baggage. It comes with living."

He sounded cavalier about it, but she knew he wasn't. "I want you so badly, I'm shaking in anticipation."

"Me, too." He urged her inside his bedroom and closed the door softly behind them. The blinds were open and the moon was nearly full. Slatted moonlight cut across the room.

Ash reached for the hem of her sweater and tugged it over her head. Once that was off, he knelt and removed her leather boots, then went to work on the closure of her jeans. When she was down to her underwear, he stood back, raking her body with a heated gaze. "My God, you're beautiful."

Holly didn't consider herself beautiful, though she knew she was photogenic. "Not as beautiful as you," she whispered in a shaky voice.

He smiled wryly. "Men aren't beautiful."

She reached out and worked her hands beneath his sweatshirt. He was too tall for her to pull it off his body, but he helped, grasping the tee he wore beneath it, as well. "See?" she said. "You have a beautiful body and a face that's extremely easy to look at." She reached up to caress his chest, which made him shudder. "I love your brain, too." Her fingers moved down to unbuckle his belt, then undo his jeans. "And other things." She pressed against the erection straining beneath the zipper before she eased it down carefully.

"Tell you what," he said, breathing heavily. "I'll take care of what's left for me to take off and you can do likewise, unless you'd like me to finish what I started."

She nodded. Her own breathing came so hard and quick, she could hardly speak. "I want your hands on me, Ash. Everywhere."

He was out of his jeans, boxer shorts, boots, and socks so quick it almost made her head spin. When he started to reach around her to undo her bra, she said, "Front closure."

He kissed her first, pulling her hard against his engorged penis, then leaned back to unhook the bra.

She shrugged out of it and it fell onto the growing pile of clothing at their feet.

Ash leaned down to take one of her breasts in his mouth, murmuring, "So beautiful, Holly." He paid equal attention to the other breast, then went down on his knees, kissing his way to her navel. He peeled off her cotton briefs and slid his hand between her legs. "You're ready for me."

"How could I not be?" she responded, surprised when he picked her up and laid her on the bed.

"I want to be inside you, Holly, but I also want to taste every inch of you."

Mindless with desire, Holly said, "Do whatever you want. I'm with you all the way."

Ash covered her body with his, lavishing more attention on her breasts.

Beneath him, Holly writhed, searching for the part of him that would make her complete.

Moments later, he entered her.

She'd never experienced an orgasm before, so she hadn't known what to expect, but when it came, she moaned, and then she screamed. She tried to hold it back, but couldn't.

Ash, however, knew what to do. He caught the scream with his mouth and his tongue imitated what was happening between them.

She knew exactly when he came. He shuddered, his body trembled, and he moaned her name over and over again. Holly couldn't believe it when she came again.

How was that even possible?

Holly rolled over to face Ash, who was sound asleep, and no wonder. He'd been gone for three days doing search-and-rescue, then he'd spent most of the night loving her.

It wasn't that she didn't like spooning with him, but she wanted to do more than feel his body pressed against hers. She wanted to watch him, even if he was sleeping. She wanted to see his expression when he opened his eyes and found her in bed with him. The eyes were the windows of a person's soul. They'd tell her immediately if he regretted the hours they'd spent together, or he if was ready for more. Like she was.

When Holly woke again, it was dark as sin in the room. The almost-full moon had passed over, taking the moonlight with it. That meant it had to be close to six a.m.

She could no longer see Ash's face clearly, but she could feel his breath whispering across her skin. Every once in a while, he twitched, and once, he moaned. Was he dreaming about her? Moments later, his johnson sprang to life and pressed firmly against her belly. She smiled. He *must* be dreaming about her, just as she'd dreamed about him.

Satisfied that she didn't have to get up yet, she dozed off again, making a mental note to her brain to wake up in an hour and head back to the cottage.

Ash woke and stretched, reaching for Holly at the same time, but Holly was no longer in the bed beside him.

He reared up, searching the room, then climbed out from under the covers stark naked. Her clothes were gone, but he found his folded neatly on top of the dresser. He glanced at the clock, surprised to find it was just past nine. How long had she been gone? Or was she?

He pulled on his boxers and left the bedroom, hoping she hadn't gone further than the kitchen. On the way, he looked in on Hank, but both his son and Blaze were gone and the bed was made. "Damn," he swore softly. She'd still been there when Hank woke up.

Either she'd slept late, or Hank had woken early. Regardless, as Hank's father, he'd somehow have to explain about Holly being there that early in the morning.

After checking every room, he tore back to the bedroom, took a quick shower, and dressed, then bolted through the house, headed for the back door. He had to get to the cottage and quick.

He literally skidded to a stop when he found Hank and Blaze waiting for him in the kitchen. "'Bout time you got up, Daddy. We've been holding breakfast on you and we're starving."

"I imagine you are. I take it we're eating at Holly's?"

Hank nodded, studying his father. "I came in to wake you up and saw Holly in your bed. She said you had a sleepover."

Ash froze. "What else did she say?"

"She said you slept like a rock."

"Anything else?"

"Nope. Oh, wait! She said you don't snore."

Ash shook his head, relieved she hadn't said anything

more. "Good to know. What did you two fix for breakfast?"

Hank grinned and rubbed his belly. "French toast, with strawberries on top. It's Holly's favorite breakfast."

Ash scooped up his son for a morning hug. "We'd better get over to the cottage, then."

Hank pulled back, staring into his father's eyes. "Holly's sad."

"She is?" All kinds of thoughts ran through Ash's mind, but most of them centered on her being disappointed in his sexual prowess.

Hank nodded. "Someone called her on the phone and after that, she got sad."

A wave of anxiety swept through Ash. "Did she say who it was?"

"No."

"If she's sad, we'll have to cheer her up, won't we?"

Hank nodded. "She wants to go sledding at Christmas Valley Inn. She doesn't believe they really have reindeer in the barn."

"That's what we'll do, then." He raised his hand to knock on the cottage door, but Hank opened it and barged in, yelling. "We're here!"

Holly came out of the kitchen, smiling. "Good morning."

"Good morning," Ash replied. "Sorry I kept you two waiting." He pulled her close and kissed her. "God, what a night."

"It sure was," she agreed. "Hank, go wash your hands, sweetie, and don't touch Blaze again before you eat, okay?"

Hank nodded and ran to the laundry room.

"Can you come for another sleepover tonight?"

"I wish I could," she said, "but something's come up."

As brush-offs went, it didn't have much going for it. "I see."

"You don't, but I—"

"Let's eat," Hank said, tugging on Holly's sweater.

She glanced down at him with a big smile. "Let's do!" She looked back at Ash. "Let's talk about it later, okay?"

Ash nodded, but he didn't like what he saw in her eyes. He didn't like it one little bit.

Chapter 15

Over breakfast, they planned their day. After they ate, Ash called and confirmed the hillside was ripe for sledding and the reindeer were ready for visitors.

"I've never seen a reindeer," Holly said, setting one vase of mums back in the center of the table.

"Never?" Hank cried. "They're so pretty and they really, really like me."

"I'm sure they do, since they belong to Santa, and Santa really, really likes you, too."

"How do you know?" Hank asked with wide eyes.

"Santa likes all children," Holly said. "Doesn't he bring you presents on Christmas morning?" She hoped Hank was old enough to remember his last Charismas.

Apparently, he wasn't sure. "Did Santa bring me presents last Christmas?"

"He sure did," Ash said. "He brings you presents every Christmas."

"Wow!" Hank frowned. "How does he know what to bring?"

"You tell him."

"I *see* Santa?"

"We should find out when he's going to be in town," Holly said. "I'd like to see him, too."

They made plans to leave for the Christmas Valley Inn at one-thirty. "Kris and Nick invited us to stay for dinner," Ash said.

"That's nice," Holly said, though she wasn't sure how she felt about socializing with more people she didn't know. Not that Micah and Sylvie, and Betsy, and Livvy weren't friendly and nice, but she needed some time to think, which reminded her that she also needed to contact her attorney. "I'll walk over when it's time to go."

Ash took the hint. "Grab your coat, Hank."

"Aw, can't I stay here?"

"You and I have some research to do," Ash said.

"Research? What's that?"

"We'll look up Santa's pre-Christmas schedule."

Hank brightened over that. "Can Blaze come with us?" he asked Holly.

"Sure."

As soon as the door closed behind them, she went to the art room and pulled out her phone to call Regina Freeman. "Hi, Gina. It's Holly."

"Holly! I wondered how long it would be until I heard from you. How was your drive to Christmas Valley?"

"Relaxing and, oh, my God, Gina! You should see this place. It's straight off a Christmas card. I hope you can come visit me sometime."

"I might just do that. Evan told me I'm 'too boring,' to which I responded that it was 'better than being a butt-hole,' and that, as they say, was *The End* of our relationship. For better or for worse, I now have a lot of free time on my hands."

"Evan is an idiot. And a jerk."

"I know, but…ah, hell. To tell you the truth, I've felt

nothing but relief since he told me he found himself a fun girlfriend. Our ideas of *fun* are like night and day, and no matter what, I'll never start taking drugs."

Gina's brother had overdosed on drugs, so Holly understood. Only by the grace of God had he survived and gone on to live a productive life. "Is everything settled with the house sale and the estate sale?"

"Pretty much. The couple buying your house is filthy rich and they made a cash offer."

"Did you get along all right with Abercrombie Jones?"

"He's okay, but a little stuffy. I worked with him once before, so I knew how to handle him this time."

Holly laughed. "Thank goodness."

Gina agreed. "Now that we have all the sale chit-chat out of the way, are you calling about Jarrett?"

"Yes."

"How'd you find out?"

"I'm on a text notification list from the parole board."

"Me, too. I don't know what to say, Holly. That dickwad is the kind of guy who should spend his life in prison, not get out on parole after seven years."

"I couldn't agree more. Too bad the judge stipulated at his sentencing that he'd be eligible for parole."

"Thank God, that judge retired. I almost puked when I read the appeal paperwork Jarrett's attorney submitted, and then the bastard contacted me."

"He contacted you? Why?"

"Jarrett's been a model prisoner, blah, blah, blah, and he wants to get back together with you."

Holly barked out an incredulous laugh. "He must still be smoking crack! There's no way in hell I want him within a thousand miles of me."

"I told his lawyer that, and he informed me Jarrett has it on good authority you're still pining for him."

"Pining for him to go to hell, maybe. What do I have to do to make sure he stays in prison?"

"It's not completely up to you, Holly. The other reason he's in prison is the couple he beat to within an inch of their lives. All three of you have an opportunity to speak to the parole board."

"Would Jarrett be in the room?"

"Yes."

"Is there no other way?"

"You can send something in writing, but I'm telling you here and now, being there in person is far more effective than sending a letter."

"His hearing is the Monday after Thanksgiving. That's just over two weeks away."

"I know. Can you fly back?"

"Yeah, but I need to think about this. I'm not sure I want to testify in person."

"Not to be morbid, but I don't know what there is to think about. If he gets out, he'll find you, and you might not walk away alive this time."

Leave it to Gina to be blunt *and* morbid. "I've haven't told a soul except you where I am."

"Any private investigator could track you, Holly. You don't have a name change, you have credit cards, and you're a familiar face to half the world."

Holly's insides clenched in dismay. "You're scaring me, Gina."

"Good. Unless this creep stays in prison, you *should* be scared, and you should also be on your guard, and I mean twenty-four/seven."

Holly glanced out the window toward the house Ash shared with his son. "I've met someone."

"I'm not surprised. He's probably seen you in dozens of ads."

"He did say I looked familiar, but I told him I get that a lot." She sighed. "He's a single dad with the most adorable three-year-old boy."

"Oh, Holly."

"I know. Don't lecture me, okay?"

"Sweetie, that's the last thing I'm going to do, but I will urge you to be cautious. If you really care about this guy and his kid, think about their well-being while you're deciding how you're going to deal with Jarrett's parole hearing. And after that, think about the possibility of him walking the streets again and going after someone you care about, because you didn't speak at his hearing."

Gina's warning sent a shaft of fear down Holly's spine.

"If it was up to me, I'd put a contract out on him myself, but I don't like the idea of spending the rest of my life in prison." Gina sighed. "Call me back tomorrow and let me know what you've decided. Either way, I'll support you."

"You're a good friend, Gina. Thank you." She hesitated. "I think Ash is the man I've been waiting for."

"Ash, huh? What's the kid's name?"

"Hank. He's crazy about Blaze."

"Hank. That's a big name to grow into."

"He has a good role model. His dad is a former Navy SEAL and he runs Mountain Search-and-Rescue here."

"Where's the mom?"

"She was having an extra-marital affair and she and her boyfriend died in a snowmobile crash on Mount Beady."

"Hunh."

"Come for Christmas, Gina. I have plenty of room for you in the cottage."

"Cottage? OMG, Holly, you are well and truly countrified! Does this mean you found your Christmas spirit again?"

"Not completely, but I'm working on it." She smiled, though Gina couldn't see it. "We're going sledding this afternoon at a place called Christmas Valley Inn, and it has reindeer."

"Reindeer? I am *definitely* booking a ticket and you'd

better damned well have a Christmas tree up when I get there."

A Christmas tree. Holly hadn't thought that far ahead, but she suddenly realized a tree was exactly what she needed to help her recapture her Christmas spirit.

Rufus and Dinah

Dinah shook her head with dismay. "Why didn't we know about this Jarrett person?"

Rufus gazed upward, frowning. "Someone Upstairs messed up."

"Maybe he's no longer relevant to Holly's life."

"I doubt that. If he's in prison for something he did to Holly and two other people, he's definitely relevant." He glanced at Dinah. "Feel like taking a field trip while Holly and Ash and Hank have their afternoon at Christmas Valley Inn?"

"I'm with you. Are you thinking we need a little help here?"

"Maybe."

"Good grief! Please don't tell me you want to call Felix in again. Last time we had to turn to him for help, we almost ended up with our wings clipped."

Rufus *harrumphed*. "That's an exaggeration, Dinah, and you know it."

"You have selective memory, Rufus. Do you not remember the thunderous response from Upstairs *and* the lightning bolts."

"Vaguely," he said with a wave of his hand. "The thing is, Felix isn't afraid of anything, which makes him the right choice to infiltrate a prison."

Dinah stared at him. "Infiltrate a prison? That's insane!"

"Not really."

She remained silent for a least a minute, which was almost like an eternity in guardian angel time. "You're absolutely right, Rufus, and you're brilliant! I didn't know you had it in you."

"Of course, I'm brilliant, Dinah. Did you think I was a dolt?'

Her eyes lowered to study his lips. "I definitely don't think you're a dolt."

His own gaze dropped to study her lips. "I think another kiss is in order, don't you?"

She nodded, but didn't want to give in too easily. "Maybe after we transport ourselves."

"Maybe," he said, leaning forward to capture her in his arms. "Or maybe not."

A moment later, lips locked, they were on their way.

Chapter 16

Sledding was so much fun, Holly never wanted it to end. She also liked the saucer, but what she really liked was riding down the hillside on the large sled, with Ash behind her and Hank in her lap.

Afterward, Nick Kringle escorted them to the barn to meet the reindeer. Hank, it turned out, knew them all by name. "Vixen isn't here right now," he explained in a serious tone, "'cuz she likes to hang out at Ryker's ranch with her reindeer boyfriend."

"Really?" Holly said, her astonishment only half-feigned. "I never thought about the reindeer having boyfriends or girlfriends."

Ash grinned. "Ryker's wife, Jani, will be happy to share the story of Vixen with you."

"I'm sure I'll enjoy hearing it." She glanced at Nick. "Is it a lot of work taking care of Santa's reindeer?"

Nick laughed. "They all mind pretty well, except for Vix, but we've gotten used to her wandering ways, so she's not much of a problem anymore."

"Does Santa stop by here, or do the reindeer fly to the North Pole to hook up to the sleigh?" Holly asked.

Nick's eyes twinkled. "It can happen either way."

Holly got it then. Nick Kringle was speaking for Hank's benefit. "What about Rudolph?"

"Rudy was a figment of a Sears and Roebuck marketing person's imagination. Of course, that doesn't mean we don't have room for him, if he should ever happen to drop by."

Holly liked how Nick remembered a three-year-old hung on his every word. She also was impressed with the animals. "They're beautiful."

"We think so and the kids who come out love to see them." He glanced at Ash. "Santa will be here on December first. Invitation only."

"Thanks," Ash said, even as Hank jumped up and down, clapping and *yaying*.

"Let's head inside," Nick said. "Kris has a nice fire going and dinner should be about ready. Lachlan and Joss and the grandkids are joining us."

"Goody!" Hank cried. He looked up at Holly. "The grandkids are Lainie and baby Noah."

Inside, it was toasty warm and everyone was welcoming. Nick and Kris's grandchildren were beautiful and Holly itched to hold Noah, who was sixth months old. Joss apparently noticed and handed the baby over.

Over dinner, Kris said to Ash, "Joss and I are going to make Thanksgiving dinner this year. We'd love to have you and Hank join us. I already asked your mom."

Ash smirked. "I supposed she's bringing what's-his-name."

Kris grinned. "She is."

Ash shook his head, smiling. "We'll be here."

She glanced at Holly. "We hope you'll join us, too."

"Thank you. It sounds lovely," Holly said. "Can I let you know?"

"Sure. We always have plenty of food."

"No kidding," Joss said, which made her husband laugh.

Holly stared at him for a moment, trying to think where she'd seen him before. "I think I know you."

"You know who I *used* to be," he said, "and I'm pretty sure I know you, too."

Joss looked back-and-forth, from Holly to Lachlan and back to Holly. "*That's* why I recognized you."

"Anyone care to let me in on the secret?" Ash asked, looking puzzled.

"Secret is the key word," Holly said, caught in a trap of her own making.

"You can trust us, Holly," Kris said. "Mum's the word in this family. Because of Lach's past career, that's the way we like it."

Holly debated her hostess's sincerity, then looked at Ash, who offered some encouragement with four words. "Everyone has a past."

Maybe now was the right time. "Mine was forced on me by my mother, who thought I should enter a beauty contest when I was eleven, and a modeling competition when I was fifteen. Somewhere along the way, someone stuck the name Sophisti-Kitty on me, which I hated. When my mom died a few months ago, I walked away from modeling and I'm never going back. I hated every minute of it."

"Sophisti-Kitty," Ash said, as if tasting the word. "That's why you looked familiar. You're on the cover of one of the magazines in the rack at the grocery checkout this month." He squinted at her hair.

"But she's no longer blonde, and she no longer has hair that never quits," Joss said. "I love the *real* you, Holly."

"Thank you," Holly said, pleased by a compliment.

"What brought you to Christmas Valley?" Lachlan asked.

"When my mother took over my life, I lost my Christmas spirit. I came here to find it."

A hush fell over the group seated around the table as they contemplated her revelation.

"My mommy wasn't nice, either," Hank said, drawing a shocked glance from his father. "I'll help you find your Christmas spirit again, Holly."

"I'd love that, Hank. Thank you."

He flashed her another of his angelic smiles, which melted her heart and made her want to cry.

All these years, and she'd never realized how much goodness there was in the world, if only you knew how to find it.

Hank was in bed and sound asleep by seven-thirty.

Holly sat next to Ash on the floor, sipping hot chocolate, staring into the fire.

"I hope you'll go to Thanksgiving dinner with us at the Inn," Ash said.

"If I'm in town, I'd love to."

That threw him for a moment. "Why wouldn't you be?"

"Something's come up." She sighed and sipped from her cup. "My life is complicated, Ash, despite every attempt I've made to uncomplicate it."

"Tell me what's going on, sweetheart. Maybe I can help."

"I don't see how that's possible."

He sighed, but his voice was laced with steel when he said, "Don't underestimate me, Holly."

It took Holly five days to decide whether or not to confide in Ash. Whether or not her decision was a wise one was yet to be determined.

The problem was, the rest of her story wasn't as tame as entering beauty pageants and modeling competitions.

She took a deep breath. Hank was sound asleep and Ash sat beside her on the sofa with his arm around her shoulders. "Eight years ago, I met a man who swept me off my feet and into his bed. I ended up pregnant and my mother insisted we had to get married, because it wouldn't look right for a famous model to have a baby out of wedlock. Two days into the marriage, he showed his true colors. He was a mean sonofabitch and he liked to use his fists to prove it."

Beside her, Ash stiffened.

"After our wedding night, he didn't want to have sex with me because I looked grotesque. That was fine by me, because all I wanted to do was focus on the baby. I fixed up the nursery, and I had fun doing it. Then Jarrett would come home and criticize everything I'd done." She hesitated, because the memories were still difficult to deal with. "I did everything I could not to antagonize him. He cheated on me with other women. I knew it, but I never called him on it, because I didn't want him touching me that way ever again." She sucked in a harsh breath. "When anything in his life went bad, he took it out on me. One night, I'd had enough of him coming in stinking of booze and other women's cologne. I told him I wanted a divorce."

Ash's tightened his arm around her. "How did he take that?"

"Not well. He slapped me several times with an open palm, then he switched to using his fist, and then he threw me against the wall." Her voice dropped to a whisper. "He picked me up and did it again. Three times." Tears leaked from her eyes. How could they not when she thought about that horrible night?

"Did you call the cops?"

"After he left, I managed to crawl over to my phone. I could feel something wasn't right with my baby. I honestly didn't care about myself, but the little boy inside me was a different matter."

Ash put his mug down and covered her hands with his free one.

"The police came, and the ambulance came, but Jarrett had taken off, with a gun. I was afraid he was going to come back and use it on me because he was so angry." She gulped. "There was blood everywhere. The EMTs told me it was touch-and-go for my baby." She shook her head. "I prayed so hard for him to be all right, but…he wasn't. Jarrett had killed him and he nearly killed me. I almost bled to death before they got me to the ER."

Ash swore softly.

"After he left our house, he held up a mom-and-pop convenience market. The couple who owned it were well into their sixties and they were always there together. I shopped there regularly, even though their prices were higher than the grocery store, because they were nice people. For some reason, Jarrett fixated on that, and he was determined to make them pay for existing." She swiped at her tears and went on. "He beat them both senseless with that gun. Mr. Wentworth lost the sight in his left eye and Mrs. Wentworth ended up with a fractured skull, all because of me."

"Don't take the blame for what your husband did."

She glanced up at him, hoping her expression didn't reflect her inner turmoil. "That's easier said than done."

Ash looked like he wanted to argue, but instead, he sighed and said, "I know."

Those two simple words told her a lot about him and his past with Alicia.

"Was he arrested?"

"Yes. He went to trial and was convicted and sent to prison for twenty years, but the thing is, he's up for parole now. He's supposedly been a model prisoner and he has a crackerjack lawyer. The hearing is the Monday after Thanksgiving and my attorney thinks I should be there to speak out against his release."

"I can see why. Personal testimony is a lot more effective than written testimony."

"He screamed at me in court the day the verdict was brought in. He said, 'Next time I see you, I'm going to fucking kill you, Kitty.'" She glanced up at Ash again. "He meant it, too."

"I'll go with you."

Holly panicked. "You can't!"

"The hell I can't."

"Why would you want to?"

"Because." For a moment he remained silent, then he said, "I love you, Holly. That should be reason enough."

"Oh, Ash."

"I know. Crazy, huh?'

"No, it's just…." She didn't now how else to say it except the same way he had. "I love you, too, but if Jarrett is released, he'll find me and he'll hurt me again, but worse than that, he'll take his anger out on you and Hank, and I can't risk letting that happen."

Chapter 17

Ash's expression grew stormy. "I can take care of myself and my son," he said, "and I'm great at multitasking, which means I can damned well take care of you, too."

"But you shouldn't be put in a position where you have to."

"Holly, I'm thirty-five years old. I spent ten years fighting evil in the hellholes of the world. I'm not afraid of it."

"But you didn't have Hank then. You have to think about him now."

"I am thinking about him. He loves you. How do you think he'd feel if something happens to you?"

She jumped up from the sofa and began to pace back-and-forth in front of the fireplace. "I never should've come here. It was selfish of me not to think of anyone but myself." She came to a standstill in front of him. "I never imagined he'd come up for parole. I thought he'd spend the full twenty years in prison, and maybe die there."

"Maybe he *should* see you again. He'll show his true colors and the parole board will deny him parole."

"That's the fairy-tale ending," she shot back bitterly. "I'm not destined to have that. Ever."

Ash pushed up off the sofa, taking her in his arms.

For a moment, Holly forgot the turmoil her life was in and basked in his love for her.

Was it really true? Could two people fall in love so quickly?

"Let's turn in," he suggested.

Turn in. Nice euphemism for hit-the-sack-and-screw-all-night. Well, why not? She didn't have that many more nights with him ahead of her, because once she showed up at the parole board hearing, she was *not* coming back to Christmas Valley. To do so would expose Ash and Hank to a threat they never could have imagined.

She glanced up at him. "That's a great idea." Ash could make her forget everything for a while. Tomorrow, during the daylight hours, she could dredge it all up again, but tonight was for them. Two lovers getting to know each other better. Two lovers loving. Two lovers, period.

He lowered his head and kissed her like she was riding off to face the guillotine and there wasn't a damned thing he could do about it.

Funny as it seemed, that was exactly where it felt like she was headed.

"Holly?" Hank whispered, poking her.

Her eyes jerked open. "What's wrong?" she whispered back.

"Blaze is gone."

She blinked a few times, hoping for clearer vision, and clarity. "Gone?"

Hank nodded and his lower lip trembled. "He was sleeping on the floor next to my bed and now he's not."

"Well, he can't let himself outside, so he has to be in the house, right?"

Hank conceded that with another nod. "Will you help me find him?"

"Sure. Run put on some slippers and I'll be right there."

He turned and ran toward the door.

Holly, on the other hand, remained frozen in the bed until she was sure he was out of the room. What was she supposed to wear? Ash didn't strike her as the type of man who had a bathrobe hanging in the closet. Then she got an idea. She threw back the covers, being as quiet as possible so she wouldn't waken the man she loved. She found her briefs on the floor and pulled them on. Then she found the tee shirt he'd worn under his sweater and decided that would cover her well enough. As it turned out, it hung down to mid-thigh, providing all the cover she needed. She left the bedroom, following the sound of Hank's sniffling down the hall and into the living room.

"Blaze isn't here," he said, "and he's not in the kitch-en."

Holly decided to check for herself. A moment later, she discovered what Hank hadn't noticed. The door leading out to the patio was open about an inch. No wonder it was freezing-ass cold in the house.

She knew darned good and well Ash had closed and locked the door after letting Blaze in for the night. "Hank?" she whispered. "Go wake up your daddy."

"Why?"

"Please, don't argue, sweetie. Just go get him."

Ash was sitting up in bed, trying to figure out where

Holly was when Hank tore into the room.

"Daddy, come quick. Blaze is gone and Holly sent me to get you."

Ash rolled his eyes, thinking his son was overreacting. Where could Blaze have gone? Nowhere. Dogs didn't know how to open locked doors. "Simmer down, buddy. I'm coming."

"Hurry, Daddy! Holly is scared."

Given that his son was some kind of genius when it came to reading human emotion, Ash leapt from the bed and scrounged for his boxers, which he finally found sticking out from under the bed. He stepped into them, then Hank grabbed his fingers and urged him down the hall.

When the reached the kitchen, the blast of cold air from the open door sent his skin directly into goose-bump mode. In two long strides, he reached the door and called out, "Holly?"

No answer.

"She only had on your undershirt, Daddy. She'll be too cold outside."

Only his undershirt? Ash flew back to the bedroom, flipping on the light switch as he entered. He took a quick inventory of his clothes and hers and discovered his tee shirt and her cotton briefs were the only items missing.

His blood ran cold. Holly wouldn't go outside bare-foot, with hardly anything on. She'd come back and put on her jeans and sweater, and her socks. He jerked on his own jeans and ran back to the kitchen. Her boots were still by the back door. His blood turned to ice crystals. Where the hell was she?

He turned on the porch light and discovered it was snowing again. Her feet were bare and the patio had been devoid of snow when she'd arrived earlier that evening because he'd shoveled it. His gaze dropped to the patio.

Booted footprints had been left behind by someone who wasn't Holly.

"Daddy?'

Ash backed up the way he'd come and closed the door, careful not to touch the door handle. He picked up Hank and carried him back down the hall to the master bed-room, where his phone lay on the nightstand. Rock Dennison, his second-in-command at Mountain Search-and-Rescue, also happened to be a detective for the Christmas Valley Sheriff's Department.

He glanced at the clock. One-oh-four a.m.

"Dennison," Rock growled.

"It's me," Ash said. "Holly's gone missing. I think she's been kidnapped."

Under normal circumstances, his friend might have tossed back a tease, such as, *Are you sure she didn't just get tired of you?* However, he must have heard the urgency in Ash's tone, because he got straight to the point. "Tell me."

"Apparently, Hank woke up and discovered Blaze was gone, so he came to tell Holly, who went to check, and then she sent Hank to wake me up and bring me back. By the time I got to the kitchen, she was gone. The back door was standing wide open and there are boot prints on the patio, but no barefoot prints."

"Be there in fifteen," Rock said and the line went dead.

True to his word, Rock arrived fifteen minutes later, as did Sheriff John Pulkinen, and Deputy Sheriff Mike Aaronson. The three men used flashlights to examine the walkway and driveway as they made their way up to the house.

Unbelievably, Blaze trailed behind them.

Hank clung to Ash's leg, crying because both Blaze and Holly had disappeared.

Blaze barked and ran ahead of the three men. When he reached the doorway, Hank hugged him, but his tears renewed. "Where's Holly?"

Ash did his best to calm his son, but he was damned worried, too. Holly was too sensible to head outside, wearing practically nothing, when it was only twenty-five degrees outside.

His first conclusion had been correct. Someone had taken her against her will.

Holly was more angry than frightened, though the look on Jarrett's face had her leaning in the direction of scared shitless.

"Surprised to see me?" he snarled about four inches from her face.

"You could say that," she replied, cursing the waver her in voice.

He laughed. "I ain't ever goin' back to prison, Kitty."

Holly would have killed him then and there if she'd had a weapon. As it was, her brain would have to suffice as her weapon of choice. There *had* to be a way out of this. "Why didn't you wait for your parole hearing?"

He slapped her hard. "You think I didn't know you'd show up to testify? The people I thought I left for dead planned to, even after my attorney offered them a lot of money to stay away. I knew if they were hell-bent on being there, you would be, too. You'd cry your stupid alligator tears and get the parole board on your side, and I'd have another thirteen years in that stinkin' place. There was no fucking way I was gonna wait around for that. I saw an opportunity and I took it."

"Did you kill someone on your way out?"

He laughed like she'd just told the world's funniest joke. "So what if I did?" He leaned forward and literally growled in her face. "I like hurting people, and when you like something, you gotta keep it up." To prove his point, he grabbed her breast and squeezed so hard she cried out. "When I'm finished with you, Kitty, you'll be begging me to kill you and I'll take pleasure in it. After that, I'm headed for a place where no one will ever find me."

Holly recoiled from his bad breath, unable to imagine that he was smart enough to disappear where he couldn't be found. After he'd beat her and killed their baby, then robbed the mom-and-pop market and beat the Wentworths senseless, he'd been easy to find. She even remembered the Assistant DA handling the case telling her that most criminals made their job easier because they weren't that smart.

He rubbed her cheek with his fingertips, then slapped her again. "Oh, yeah, I forgot to mention, I'm gonna take care of the Wentworths, too, like I should'a done the first time around."

She held back a nasty retort, asking instead, "Who helped you escape?"

"You ever heard of prison groupies?" He straightened and grinned. "I got several, including one inside the fucking prison. She ain't as good-looking as you, but she's a helluva lay. She'll do anything I want, no matter what."

Holly's mouth responded before her brain had a chance to control it. "She must not have any brains, if she helped you."

His expression altered from nasty to hideous. "She's got a brain, all right, which is more than I can say for you. You'll never learn to keep your fucking mouth shut, will you?" He raised his fist and aimed it directly at Holly's face.

She braced for the impact, but at the last second, tilted her head, causing the blow to lose some of its steam. Holly took advantage of the situation and decided to play unconscious.

If there was one thing she knew about Jarrett, it was that he liked his victims kicking and screaming, not out cold. It would give her time to think and maybe figure out a way to get herself out of her predicament.

The sound of him slamming the door of wherever he'd taken her served as an exclamation point to her determination. Not too long after, an engine started up.

For the moment, at least, she counted herself safe.

Rufus and Dinah

Dinah planted her hands on her guardian angel hips and glared at Rufus. "Why didn't you tell me Holly was going to be kidnapped?"

Rufus went nose-to-nose with Dinah. "Because I didn't know, that's why."

"First, we didn't know about Jarrett, and then we didn't know he'd kidnap her. This is an untenable situation, Rufus."

"I know, I know," her heavenly counterpart grumbled, pacing back-and-forth in midair.

"How are we going to get her out of this?" Dinah asked, her tone so emotional, Rufus hardly recognized it.

"We're not."

"But…but…."

"Ash and Holly herself are going to get her out of this mess."

"*What?*"

"You heard me, Dinah."

"I heard you, all right, but I can't believe it. We *never*

stand by when something like this happens to our humans."

"Well, this time, we do."

"Says who?"

He pointed upward.

Dinah gasped. "That can't be right!"

He slipped an arm around her shoulders, but she jerked away.

"Just because I enjoy kissing you, Rufus, doesn't mean I'm going to stand by and watch that maniac do something horrible to Holly that could scar her for the rest of her life, or worse."

"You don't have any choice. Surely, you know that?"

Dinah began to pace on the peak of the roof. She had impeccable balance, so it came as a surprise when she lost her footing and tumbled down over the ragged composition shingles of the old cabin and into the snow, flat on her face.

"See what I mean?" Rufus said, standing over her. "When the Big Guy wants things his way, things like you falling off the roof happen."

Dinah rolled over, her eyes filled with tears and her mouth full of snow. She swiped at her eye
s and spit out the snow. "I never thought I'd say this, but I don't agree with the Big Guy this time. Period. End of story. Are you going to help me save Holly or not?"

Rufus shrugged and held out his hand to her. "Or not."

"Ooohhh." She ignored his hand and a moment later, she was gone.

Unable to believe she'd vanish like that before they were through discussing things, Rufus cried out, "Dinah, wait! What did you have in mind?"

Chapter 18

Ash called Lachlan and Joss, even though it was the middle of the night. "Holly's been kidnapped. Can I bring Hank over while we search for her?"

"Absolutely."

Ten minutes later, he dropped his son off with the Kringles, who were his closest neighbors.

"Anything I can do to help?" Lachlan asked, taking Hank in his arms.

"Do you mind dog-sitting Holly's dog, too?"

"Not at all."

"Let me know if you organize a search party, or whatever," Joss said. "I'll get a phone chain going."

Ash nodded, and said, "Don't worry, Hank. We'll find her."

Hank's little head bobbed, but he continued to cry.

Ash felt horrible about leaving his son, but he couldn't just sit around waiting for news of Holly to come to him.

He had to find her, and he had to find her alive.

That stopped him in his tracks. Finding Holly wasn't

like his other search-and-rescue operations, where he focused on only one goal, rescue or recovery. This situation was entirely different. This was about Holly.

He couldn't be objective because he loved her. He wanted to marry her, have more children with her, and live the rest of his life with her. He might be able to tamp down his anxiety and stress, but how the hell was he supposed to quell the *what-ifs* swimming around in his head?

What if whoever had taken her killed her?

What if he did horrible things to her before he killed her?

What if she'd gone willingly with whoever had her?

What if she was completely off her rocker because she'd lost her baby?

What if she only loved him because he had a kid?

He swore softly, but pungently. What the hell was wrong with him? Holly hadn't kept what Jarrett had done to her a secret because she wanted to hide it from him. She'd kept it a secret because she was trying to outrun her past. Hell, if he didn't have Hank, he might have run, too, after Alicia died. In fact, in a way, he was running, but he was doing it in-place, instead of somewhere else far away.

He'd sworn to himself that he'd never fall in love again. In the same breath, he'd promised he'd never marry again, not even so Hank could have a mom.

He sat down on the back bumper of his truck and put his head in his hands. He had to think. Letting all kinds of weird thoughts jumble his brain wasn't helping anything.

A hand came down on his shoulder. Ash jumped.

"It's just me," Rock said. "The sheriff talked to the prison. Apparently, Jarrett Kingston broke out on Sunday afternoon with the help of his girlfriend, the prison librarian. Typical of freaks of his ilk, he left her behind."

"I don't suppose she's given up anything useful."

"On the contrary, she's singing like the proverbial canary. Dave thinks he knows where Kingston took Holly, but we have a problem. There's a back way in, but we need your S-and-R expertise and knowledge of the terrain."

Ash recognized a manufactured invitation when he heard one, but it didn't matter. "Count me in. I'll do whatever it takes."

"You know we don't involve families in rescues."

"I'm not family, so don't worry about it."

"Technically, that's true, but you are involved."

Ash glared at his friend.

Rock flexed his jaw. "Just remember, I'm in charge, not you."

At that point, Ash would have said anything to be included. "Agreed."

"We'll need Mack Kearny and Spider Henry with us."

Ash nodded. They each knew what the others thought and what their strengths were. "We work best as a team."

"I'll call them in, and to be on the safe side, the sheriff will deputize the three of you."

"All right." Ash understood immediately why that was necessary. They were all expert marksmen and Jarrett Kingston was a wanted felon who liked to hurt people.

"Go home and get your rifle and your climbing gear. Meet back here in thirty minutes."

Ash didn't waste time discussing it. Even though he was Rock's boss on S-and-R operations, in this case, Rock was his boss. He'd learned as a SEAL, when you got an order, you followed it.

Holly curled up on the cold floor, wondering why Jarrett's girlfriend hadn't shown her face yet. After a few minutes, it occurred to her that he was such a lowlife, he'd probably abandoned her before leaving SoCal. With any luck, she was so ticked off he'd left her behind, she was already spilling her guts to the police. With even more luck, that would include his exact location.

Luck. That was something in short supply in Holly's life. Or at least, it had been until she met Ash and Hank.

After Jarrett, and what he'd done to her, causing her to lose the baby, she'd sworn off men. She never considered that she might meet another man and fall in love with him. All these years later, she had proved herself wrong.

She had one more secret she hadn't mentioned to Ash. It involved her ability to get pregnant again. The gynecologist who'd treated her in the ER had informed her that she might never be able to conceive again. If things progressed between her and Ash, and by some strange turn of events, he asked her to marry him, she knew she'd have to come clean about that. As much as he loved his son, he might not want to tie himself down to a woman who couldn't give him more children.

The thought of losing him because of that was so distressing, Holly had to mentally slap some sense into herself. *Prioritize!* her brain screamed.

On the way to wherever they were, Jarrett had informed her, in graphic detail, of his plans to assault her sexually. She knew he'd beat her as he did so, just because he could. And then he'd kill her, just because he could.

Staying alive had to be her top concern for the moment. It was imperative that she figure out how to get away from him.

She tested the bindings on her wrists, trying not to make any noise. They were loose. Could she wriggle out of them and untie her feet? It was worth a try. She listened for several moments, but heard nothing. Had he actually driven away?

Holly had no choice but to go with that assumption. It was either that, or let him do what he wanted with her when he came back, and that simply wasn't an option.

Sheriff John Pulkinen pointed to a map he'd tacked up on the cork board. "The woman who helped Kingston escape bookmarked the maps and cabin locations they'd been looking at online. She remembers that he settled on a rundown structure on this side of Mount Beady, where the old gold mine entrance is located." He glanced around the room, making eye contact with Ash, Rock, Mack, Spider, and Ryker Manning, who would transport them in his helicopter. "That structure served as a business office for the mining company, but it's been abandoned for over twenty-five years."

"As we all know," Rock said, taking over, "the south face of Mount Beady is devoid of trees at the higher elevation, primarily because it's sheer granite. The good news is, there are a couple of landing sites, and one of them happens to be above the cabin. Ryker will approach from the east and set us down at that location, which is about a thousand feet away. That should put enough distance between us and the building to keep our arrival from being heard." He scanned the small group. "I don't know that we'll need our climbing gear, but better to be over-prepared than under-prepared."

"I'll maintain contact with you," the sheriff said. "Mike and I will be about two hundred feet below the cabin, in the first stand of trees, which should offer us a little cover. Everyone checks in at fifteen-minute intervals. Got it?"

The men nodded.

"I assume you all understand what it means to be deputized."

Again, they nodded.

"If you have to shoot, make sure you hit your target, not Holly Morgan."

No one commented that she might already be dead, but Ash knew they were thinking it.

As if in confirmation, six pairs of eyes landed on him with expressions that were both compassionate and determined.

"Semper Fi," he said, glad they weren't stupid enough to offer him pity.

They responded in kind.

Holly managed to slip her hands out of the wrist restraints, though it was no easy feat. She went to work on the ankle bindings after that. That effort was more difficult because of the darkness. Plus, she was shivering. It was damned cold wearing only her briefs and Ash's tee shirt.

A noise outside threw her for a moment, but it also fueled her urgency to get out of the bindings. Fortunately for her, Jarrett had either been lazy or clumsy, or both. She located the knot, loosened it, and the binding fell away.

She crawled on her hands and knees toward the direction he'd exited the room, or at least she thought it was. It didn't occur to her that she might be headed the wrong way until her head hit the wall. She climbed to her feet and let her hands do the walking over the rough wood surface. Picking up splinter after splinter, she didn't dwell on the discomfort. If she survived, she'd have plenty of time to pluck them out, and she'd be thankful for every one of them.

After circling the entire room, she was baffled because she hadn't found a door. Determined to go around again, she worked her way to the next corner. A scraping noise sounded behind her. Holly froze.

A weak, thin beam of light penetrated the area where she'd just been. Fortunately for her, Jarrett's flashlight batteries were waning. She also realized he hadn't driven away, but must've sat in his vehicle, running the heater.

Holly pressed hard into the corner unmindful of spiders or whatever else congregated there.

Jarrett let out a howl of rage when his light landed on her bindings. "Where are you, Holly?" He aimed the flashlight at the dirt floor as he moved in the direction opposite of where she stood.

Holly had a brainstorm. Whether it would work on not, she had no idea, but she had to try. The door had opened toward her, shielding her. With her back to the wooden wall, she inched closer, moving around it with as much stealth as she could muster. In the doorway, she blinked against the glare of the snow, then quickly studied the door.

No wonder she hadn't been able to find a door knob! There wasn't one. The door had a wooden slat lock that latched from the outside.

Jarrett was on the opposite side of the room, still aiming his light where the floor met the wall. It was now or never. She grasped the latch and leaped through the opening, pushing the slat into place, securely locking the door. She didn't take time to wonder why it latched from the outside, nor did she stop to think about the adverse effects of running barefoot through the snow. All she knew was that she had to get away, and fast.

She hadn't run more than twenty feet before she noticed the cave up ahead. Or at least, she thought it was a cave. It was partially boarded up, but she didn't care. I would provide shelter, and right now, that's what she needed more than anything.

Well, except maybe to be rescued.

Chapter 19

The cold air played havoc, not only with Holly's bare extremities, but with her lungs. She reached the cave opening, gasping for breath, and yanked on one of the flat boards covering it.

It came away so easily, she found herself butt-first in the snow. She scrambled back up and peered inside the dark space. It smelled horrible, but death probably smelled worse. She yanked off one more board and crawled through the opening, not thinking about the trail she'd left behind in the snow. More concerned about spiders, snakes, and other critters, she forced herself to move further into the cave.

A few feet in, she could still see where she was going, but beyond that was total darkness. Much to her dismay, she took another step and tripped over something. She cursed softly and picked herself up off the ground. She ignored her new injuries, intent on exploring the inside of the wooden box she'd stumbled over.

Supplies in a boarded-up cave? Why?

She grasped the lantern handle, relieved when she heard the slosh of kerosene in the tank. Praying she'd also find matches in the wooden box, she began pulling things out. Someone upstairs must have been looking out for her, because she came across a small tin that contained at least a dozen wooden matches. She struck one on the outside of the wooden box, but it didn't light.

Shaking from the cold, she considered her options. She was in a cave. Caves had rock walls. She reached out with her free hand to find the cave wall, then raised her other hand and ran the match against the rock. A small flame rewarded her effort.

A moment later, the lantern was lit. She held it up, turning in a circle to examine her surroundings. Tiny sparkles winked at her. She held the lantern closer to the rock wall. Gold sparkles. Had she taken refuge in an abandoned gold mine?

She went back to examining the box. Canned goods, for which she had no can opener. A canteen, which she'd rather not drink from, since she had snow at her disposal outside the cave. Dynamite. "Dear God," she breathed. She lifted it carefully and set it aside. Beneath that was a blanket. Now that, she could use. She moved to the other side of the cave and set the lantern down, away from the dynamite, then went back for the blanket. She wrapped it around her body and turned back toward the lantern, when it suddenly dawned on her how deep the wooden box was.

After a moment's hesitation, she decided to see what remained at the bottom of the box. Much to her amazement, she discovered a package wrapped in brown paper and tied with a coarse string. She grabbed it and again moved toward the lantern, which she hoped would provide a modicum warmth.

Holly sat, pulling the scratchy wool blanket around her more securely. Several minutes later, her teeth-chattering had subsided somewhat. Her hands crept out and untied the string. She unwrapped the paper and stared at the contents in shock. A man's shirt, a pair of socks, and a pair of men's trousers. She closed her eyes and uttered a prayer of thanks.

The socks went on first. They were too big, but she considered a possible solution. She pulled the trousers on next, then stood and threaded the string through the belt loops, tying it securely so the pants wouldn't fall off. She leaned over to work the leg hems into the socks, which served to keep the cold out and the socks up. After that, she tugged on the shirt over Ash's tee, wishing she also had something to keep her head and hands warm.

An animal passed by outside the opening. All Holly could tell was that it was big and it had antlers. In a moment of whimsy, she considered inviting it in for company, and possibly to share its body heat.

Jarrett continued to scream intermittently. She didn't worry, except when he went quiet. Those times, she was certain, he was plotting his escape. Or he'd already escaped and he was creeping closer to the cave.

The wind picked up outside, blowing snow in through the opening.

Holly had warmed sufficiently to finish her search of the cave entry. She stood with the blanket around her again and grabbed the lantern, which she held away from her body. Nothing more presented, so she moved further away from the boarded-up opening. A pair of men's boots were propped up against the wall on the opposite side of what looked like a sinkhole.

She held the lantern up higher, hoping to find that the way around the hole would be wide enough for her to traverse. She *had* to get those boots. Logically, she knew if they were on her feet, she might not get frostbite.

The problem was, she knew she couldn't make it unless she removed the blanket and left the lantern behind.

Then, and only then, she was convinced she could do it. She'd throw the boots over the opening to this side, and carefully make her way back. No sweat.

Now that she had the logistics worked out, did she have the courage to try?

She weighed the options. Cold feet, probable frostbite. Warmer feet in boots, no frostbite.

The second option won, hands down.

Holly set the lantern on the ground nearest the side she'd determined had the widest access, then folded the blanket, hoping it would preserve some of her body heat for when she wrapped it around herself again. She examined her path, looking for hand-holds and committing them to memory.

She'd almost reached the other side when she made one misstep and went sailing headfirst into the sinkhole.

The trek down the granite face of Mt. Beady was treacherous because of the snow. Not that it wasn't when there was no snow, but in Ash's mind, the white stuff slowed their progress toward the gold mine, making every step all the more dangerous.

The snow began to fall harder. Already, it muffled every little sound. What if Holly cried out and they couldn't hear her?

Visibility sucked and twilight was not far off. That worried Ash most of all. Night rescues were always harder than daylight rescues. How had the entire day passed already and they still hadn't found Holly?

As they neared the abandoned mine building, they heard the echo of what sounded like an angry man screaming, but they couldn't pinpoint which direction it was coming from. Such were the vagaries of snow muffling sound.

He heard Rock check in, so he did the same. The others behind them followed suit.

God help him, but he hated not being the one in charge. It wasn't that Rock was incapable of leading them, because he was, but Ash had grown accustomed to being in charge, no matter what. It was a tough pill to swallow, being a follower, not a leader.

They did one more check-in, and ten minutes later, they were directly above and behind the abandoned structure.

A moment later, gunshots rang out.

The four men ducked, even though it was obvious they weren't being fired on. Old combat habits died hard.

Rock motioned Ash to follow him, and directed Mack and Spider to go east. All former military, they knew how to approach and crept toward the building in silence.

More gunshots rang out, exploding bits of wood outward onto the snow.

Rock moved toward the door. Ash followed. Mack and Spider appeared from the east, flanking the opposite side of the door.

"He's locked inside," Rock muttered in a hushed tone.

"How is that possible?" Mack asked.

"Holly must have gotten away from him," Ash whispered.

"Let's hope so," Spider said, equally quiet.

"Who's out there?" Kingston screamed. "I hear you, bitch. Open the goddamned door!" When no response came back, he fired two more shots. Still the door remained locked.

Ash backed away and made radio contact with the sheriff and his deputy. "Holly got away from him somehow and locked him in the building."

"Good to know," Sheriff Pulkinen replied. "Heard the gunshots, so I called for an ambulance. We're on our way up."

"Hold on until you hear from us." Ash signed off and moved back into position behind Rock. "How do you want to play this?"

"I wish to hell I knew what kind of weapon he has," Rock said. "It might tell me how many shots he has left."

"He's fired six, by my count," Mack said.

"I counted seven," Ash said.

"I think Ash is right," Spider said. "That latch lock can't be that sturdy, considering. I'll take a run at it."

"Hold on," Rock said. "I'm thinking." After a moment, he asked, "Is there a window on the east side?"

"No."

"So, he's in the dark, but he probably has a flashlight," Rock said. "I'm the only one wearing Kevlar, so I'll tackle the door. Be ready for whatever he's got."

No one argued with him. He squared off with the door, flipped up the latch, and gave the door a shove. He dropped to his belly before it was halfway open.

Gunfire split the snowy night air as shot after shot rang out. And then all was silent.

Rock stayed down.

Ash called out, "Come out with your hands up."

"Fuck you!" Kingston fired two more shots, then nothing until he screamed, "Shit!"

Ash took that as an indication that the clip in Kingston's weapon was finally empty.

Rock apparently did, too. He reared up and rushed Kingston, with Ash, Mack, and Spider close behind. In moments, Holly's kidnapper was face-first on the dirt floor and handcuffed.

Kingston fought them the entire time.

"Where's Holly?" Ash demanded.

"How the hell do I know?" Kingston screamed. "The bitch locked me in here. I swear, when I find her, I'm going to rip out her fucking eyeballs and them I'm going to fucking kill her!"

Spider and Mack pulled the guy up off the floor, while Rock radioed the sheriff to come on up.

Ash was so angry, he punched Kingston in the gut, then gave him an upper right, sending him back to the ground, unconscious.

"You two stay with him until John and Mike get here," Rock ordered.

Ash had already left the building. He stood outside, shining his light over the snow. "This way." He raced over to the entrance of the gold mine, where he and Rock pulled off the remaining boards over the opening and entered the cave. "Holly!" he yelled. "Holly!"

"You know she's in here. There's a lantern burning."

Ash nodded, but didn't waste time with words. The fear growing inside him continued to mount. Why was there a lantern and a blanket, but no Holly? He called her name one more time. No answer. He shined his light further into the cave, then lowered it. That's when he noticed the hole.

He ripped off his climbing gear and dropped to his belly, crawling forward. At the edge of the hole, he shined his light down, and there she was.

"What's going on?" John Pulkinen called from the opening.

"Holly's fallen into a sinkhole," Ash hollered, crawling backward. "If you and Mike take Kingston, that will free up my team to get her out."

The sheriff didn't question Ash, which was just as well, because he wasn't in any frame of mind to be challenged.

Moments later, Mack and Spider joined him and Rock and they formulated a plan.

Thirty minutes later, they hoisted Holly up in a makeshift stretcher they'd made from the blanket she'd left next to the lantern. Once she was secure, they pulled Ash up.

Spider stepped outside and radioed the sheriff. "Is the bus at your location?"

"Yes. Ready and waiting."

"Okay. We're bringing her down."

Holly moaned. She didn't like being jostled, and she didn't want Jarrett touching her. She began to squirm.

"Holly, it's me."

Still, she fought, struggling against Jarrett's efforts to still her.

"Holly, stop! It's me."

She opened her eyes and recognized the face of the man who had her pinned to the ground. Ash, not Jarrett. "Ash! Oh, my God, Ash."

"Don't move, sweetheart. I'm checking you for injuries."

"I hurt everywhere."

"I can imagine. You took quite a fall."

She collapsed back against the ground, completely spent, though in reality, she'd barely exerted herself. Stress, she was reminded once again, was a harsh taskmaster.

Ash dug into the backpack beside him and pulled out a plastic container with a big red X on it.

"I want you to take something for pain before I carry you down to the ambulance."

"Okay." Holly wasn't much into medications of any kind, but on the other hand, Ash probably didn't want to hear her moaning and groaning in pain, either. "Is he dead?"

"No, unfortunately. The sheriff and one of his deputies are transporting him back to town."

"I wish he *was* dead. Is that awful of me?"

"Absolutely not."

"How did you find me?" she whispered.

"The person who helped him escape told the prison officials where he was headed."

A wave of relief swept through her as if it were an emotional tsunami. "I love you so much." Before she could say more, she lost consciousness again.

"I'll carry her down," Ash said.

"I'll grab your stuff. If you want me to carry her partway, say the word. It's better to share the carry and move faster than to slow your progress while you play hero." That, from Rock, a man who wasted few words.

Ash had the urge to tell his friend to go take a jump off a high cliff, but why waste time or energy when Rock was right.

He wrapped the blanket around Holly and lifted her off the cave floor, mindful that she might have internal injuries or broken bones, praying at the same time that she didn't.

Rufus and Dinah

Angel tears streamed down Dinah's face like a mini-river. "How did we let this happen?"

Rufus snorted. "We didn't *let* it happen, Dinah. You know perfectly well there's a reason that one bumper sticker exists."

"What are you talking about now? You know I don't drive." She threw up her hands. "For that matter, neither one of us drives!"

"I'm talking about *stuff* happens. We have no control over what Jarrett Kingston does or did."

"We should have!" Dinah cried. "Holly could've died on that mountain."

"But she didn't."

"Or she could have sustained life-threatening injuries when she fell into the sinkhole."

"But she didn't."

"You don't know that!" Dinah screamed, fisting her hands. "You are so infuriating!"

"You're right, I don't, but I stand by what I said before. Holly and Ash are our charges. Jarrett Kingston isn't. We aren't allowed to interfere with his actions."

"I need to talk to the Big Guy," Dinah said. "Something has to be done about the way he runs things.

Rufus gaped at her. "You really think you're going to talk Him into changing the way He does things after all these eons."

"I can try."

"Dinah, love, save yourself the trouble and give this a more comprehensive think-through."

She unclenched her fists and her guardian angel body lifted a good twelve feet above the top of the pine tree.

Not to be outdone by her levitation, Rufus floated up so he was face-to-face with her. "Dinah," he said softly.

"Don't get all mushy on me, Rufus." She fisted her hands again. "I'm angry and I need to get it out of my system."

"I can help with that."

"Ha!"

"I can." He took one of her fists in his hands and gently pried opened her fingers. Then he took on her other fist. "See? Don't you feel better already?"

"No!"

Rufus knew she was lying. There was one more thing he could try that might help her forget about their inadequacies as guardian angels, and he wasn't above doing it. He pulled Dinah into his arms and crooned, "There, there...."

"Why does everything have to be so complicated?" she wailed softly.

"That's why they call it life. It's just the way it is."

"Life is for the living, not us."

"They have human lives and we have guardian angel lives," he said, as if she didn't already know the difference.

"Are you going kiss me, my darling, obstinate, Rufus,

or keep me in suspense?"

He chuckled. "Like you need to ask."

"Apparently, I did. Christmas is only a month away and now Holly's injured and we have so much to do before—"

Rufus cut her off mid-complaint in the only way he knew how. In some ways, he wished he'd known how pleasurable kissing was from the get-go.

If not for Dinah, he probably still wouldn't know.

His ignorance would have been bliss, but not as blissful as locking lips with her.

Chapter 20

Ash kept glancing down at Holly, even though he couldn't really see her. Darkness had settled in, the full moon was completely obscured, and it was snowing even harder than before. Spider and Mack flanked him, lighting his path. Rock forged ahead of them, doing the same thing. Still, it was slow going.

"EMTs, we're five minutes out," Rock said into his radio.

"Roger," came the reply from the ambulance.

It actually took them six minutes to reach the bus, but who was counting.

The EMTs gave Holly a cursory exam that included putting on a cervical collar before they placed her on the gurney. They got an IV started, checked her pupils and her pulse, covered her with two clean blankets, and loaded the gurney into the ambulance.

"I'm riding with her," Ash said.

"Sorry, no can do," one of the EMTs said.

Because a fire truck always responded to medical calls,

Ash knew the firefighter driving the truck, Sam Reed. The guy was one of Hank's heroes, though not strictly because his personal truck had hit an icy patch and gone off the road and down a hillside. "Sam, kindly inform this medic that I'm riding in the back, with Holly, to the hospital."

Sam smiled and put a hand on the EMT's shoulder. "Ease up, Jett. This is Ash Hammell. You're new to the Valley, so you don't know that he operates Mountain Search-and-Rescue, and you're going to be running into him a lot, if you manage to keep your job with CVFD."

Ash admired the way Sam had let the new kid on the block know his job was in jeopardy if he didn't let Ash ride along.

"Sorry, sir," Jett said. "I was told no ride-alongs. I apologize."

Ash gave him a friendly nod. "No worries, buddy. It's just that this is the woman I plan to marry, and I'm sticking to her like glue from here until the ceremony takes place."

Jett's eyes widened. "That's some serious stuff."

"Yes, it is," Ash agreed. He climbed up into the back of the ambulance without another word.

Holly came to in a bouncy house. At least, that's what it felt like, since she was being jostled. In truth, she couldn't figure out where she was. All she knew was that she hurt all over. What the heck had happened?

Bit by bit, her memory returned. Jarrett had taken her from Ash's house, mumbling about making her pay. He'd hit her and she must have passed out, because when she came to, she was in a dark place with a dirt floor and Jarrett was badgering her again, using his open palm and his fists to make his points.

Now that she thought about it, her face hurt, too, and she had a terrible headache.

She'd escaped her bindings, then searched for the door. Jarrett had come in and she'd taken advantage of sneaking around the door to lock *him* inside the building. After that, she'd run through the snow and noticed the cave. She'd ripped off two boards, gone inside, and discovered a wooden box with stuff inside and then...nothing.

She blinked a couple of times, trying to clear her vision, and examined her surroundings. Then she realized she was in an ambulance. Ash sat beside her with his eyes closed, wearing a worried expression. "Ash?"

His eyes flew open and his hold on her hand tightened. "What, baby?"

"I'm no baby."

"I know." He almost smiled. "It was a term of endearment."

She stared up at him, bemused. "Why am I in an ambulance?"

"Don't you remember what happened?"

She nodded. "I locked Jarrett in that cabin or whatever it was." The ambulance went over a bump, reminding her of her aches and pains. "Did he shoot me?"

"No."

"I hurt everywhere." Even her insides felt wrong. "I think I'm going to puke."

Ash took her at her word and snapped his fingers at the EMT, who handed over a barf bag.

"She may have a concussion," the EMT said.

"I'm sure she does," Ash said, holding her up so she could toss her cookies without choking to death.

Holly closed her eyes, humiliated that she'd hurled in front of not one, but two men who resembled Marvel Comics Super Heroes. "Jarrett hit me several times, but I got out of my restraints, and then I got out and locked him in and I ran...to the cave." She closed her eyes, trying to recover more of what had happened. "Why can't I remember what happened after that?"

"Don't talk anymore, sweetheart. Save your energy, okay?"

Holly closed her eyes again, wondering why Ash's voice seemed to be clogged with emotion.

The next time Holly awakened, she found herself in a hospital bed.

She lifted her arm to check her watch, but the only thing on her wrist was a plastic ID band identifying her. She'd only been in a hospital once. At the time, she'd been so traumatized, she barely remembered even being in the ER. What she did remember was the grief she'd experienced afterward at the loss of her precious baby boy.

She moved her head slowly, taking in her surrounds. A window, beeping machines, a dim light behind her. A tray table. A man sleeping in a chair beside the bed. Not just any man. Ash, the man she loved. He held her hand. Holly found that incredibly sweet, and comforting.

"Ash?" she said, her voice no more than a whisper. When he didn't rouse, she tried once more, again with no luck. Stymied, she decided to give his hand a squeeze.

He jumped and his body lurched forward. "Holly, thank God!" He stood and leaned over her.

Holly was ready for a kiss, but instead of him aiming for her lips, he kissed her on the forehead. "Is that all I get?" she murmured in a teasing tone.

With a gentle hand, he pushed the hair off her forehead, frowning down at her with what looked like anger.

"Did I do something to make you mad?"

"No, sweetheart. I'm pissed as hell that he hit you, that's all."

"My face hurts. Am I black-and-blue?"

"You could say that."

"Am I in the ER or the hospital?"

"The hospital."

"For how long?"

"Two days."

"Two days! Why?"

"You're injured."

"Yes, but two days? That seems like a long time to be here."

"To me, it's been an eternity."

"Do I have a concussion?"

"Yes."

She searched his eyes, looking for answers he seemed reluctant to give. "What's wrong?"

"You had surgery and you're in the ICU."

"But I'm okay."

Instead of answering, he hit the button to summon the nurse. Then he said, "I love you, Holly. I want to marry you, if you'll have me."

"I love you, too." Before she could accept his proposal, or even think about it, the door pushed open and a nurse rushed in.

"She's finally awake," Ash said.

"Good." The nurse pulled out a phone and texted someone before she checked all the beeping machines. "Her vitals look good."

A minute later, the door opened again and a man in a white coat walked in, pushing on the door so it stayed open. Holly presumed he was the doctor, which he confirmed when he introduced himself as Greyson Dixon, neurologist, "But you can call me Grey." He nodded at Ash, then continued. "Don't let the neurology thing put you off. This is a small hospital, and sometimes we fill in for each other when one of us is in the delivery room while his wife is having a baby."

"Good to know," Holly said, matching his semi-serious tone. "So, I don't need a neurologist, per se?"

He smiled, as if to reassure her, then dropped his bombshell. "I performed surgery on you. It went well, though until you woke up, we considered you touch-and-go."

"Touch-and-go? What, exactly, does that mean?"

"Do you want the long explanation, or the *Reader's Digest* version?"

"The short version is good for now. I can wait for the longer version until later."

He nodded. "Ash said you fell twice last week and again two days ago, when you toppled into that sinkhole. You had a blood clot on your brain and I removed it."

"You cut my head open?"

"We had to, but don't worry. Jeremy Fiske, who assisted me, and I both guarantee our work. You'll be up and walking around in no time, and your hair will grow back."

"You cut my hair?"

"No, we shaved away about a two-inch square of it."

Holly wanted to ask how ugly the scar would be, but she ran out of steam, and it didn't matter anyway. These days, she honestly didn't worry about her appearance.

She closed her eyes, and fell into a restful sleep, rather than unconsciousness.

Ash stared down at Holly with a worried expression. "Is she really going to be okay?"

"She really is. You've been here for two days. Go home, take a shower, get something to eat, and come back. You're starting to stink."

Ash looked over at Grey like he was a monster with a sense of humor. "Really? That's the best you've got?"

"You're not going to do her any good if you don't man up."

That made Ash laugh. "Like you would know."

"I'll take you on any day, Ash, and you know it'll be an equal match."

Ash nodded his acknowledgment. Just because Grey was a doctor, didn't mean he was a wimp. They stood eye-to-eye, and were of a similar build, not because they worked out in a gym every day, but because that's how God had doled out their bodies. "When can I take her home?"

"Not for a while. She'll be in ICU for another day, then she'll go to a room on the floor for a couple of days, and when we think she's ready to go, you can take her." He tilted his head at Ash. "What's the hurry?"

"I'm going to marry her. I need her out of here to do that."

Grey grinned. "You do know the hospital has a chaplain *and* a chapel in the building, right? We can roll her down there, no sweat."

Ash hadn't considered that, especially since he'd already reserved the Christmas Valley Inn for their nuptials because Holly had loved the place.

Of course, she hadn't said yes to his proposal, but he was confident she would, once she was wide awake again and in control of her faculties.

A *no*, on the other hand, would pretty much put a kink in the works.

Chapter 21

The doctors deemed Holly well enough to leave the hospital. As far as she was concerned, it wasn't a minute too soon.

Confinement, she realized, was not her thing, even though every one of her new friends had made a point of visiting, and none had lacked for conversation. Truth be told, she would have much rather been out of the hospital and spending time alone with Ash. In his bed.

He called at ten to make sure her release time was still ten-thirty.

"Please, hurry, in case they let me go earlier."

"I will. Hank is super excited to see you."

"I'm excited to see him, too. And Blaze."

The nurse came in just as she hung up. "I need your temp before you go."

Great. Holly was all hot and bothered thinking about her and Ash together in his bed, and now this. She hoped the mercury didn't pop through the end of the glass tube from the heat. Why couldn't the hospital use those updated forehead thermometers, like the rest of the world did?

Dr. You-Can-Call-Me-Grey came in while the thermometer was sticking out of her mouth. He smiled at her, and if she hadn't been madly in love with Ash, she might have fallen for him. As it was, he was safe for some other lucky woman.

The nurse read her temp then batted her eyelashes at the doctor, who grinned. Once the nurse had gone, Holly said, "How do you survive the constant flirting?"

"Flirting? Is that what it is?" he asked, apparently bewildered by her comment.

"Surely, you know that."

"I guess the question is, how do *you* know?"

"I've had men do the same to me. I hated it."

"Hmm. I suppose that has something to do with you being Sophisti-Kitty."

"Yes, and I'd sooner forget that, thank you." She frowned. "How come you never mentioned you know what I used to do?"

"I figured if you wanted to tell me, you would, and since you didn't, I decided you were either hiding from your public, or running away from them. From there, I deduced it was the latter and kept my yap shut."

"You're a wise man, but you just made my head spin. I have a friend I think you'd like."

For a moment, he looked horrified. "Please don't try and set me up with anyone. I'm perfectly happy with my life the way it is."

"I thought I was, too, until I met Ash."

He sighed, shaking his head. "See, that's what falling in love does to a person. Makes them think everyone else should be in love, too."

Holly didn't argue the point, though she did think her attorney, Gina, and Grey Dixon would make a good match. "I'm not asking you to marry her and have a dozen babies with her, you know. I just think you'd get along. She's happy being single, too."

The doctor blatantly ignored her explanation. "I came up to wish you a speedy recovery and to tell you I've made a follow-up appointment for you a week from tomorrow, my office, which is downstairs on the first floor. Bring the pooch. I'd love to see him."

"Better yet," Ash said from the doorway, "come to dinner tonight and spend some quality time with Blaze."

Grey turned, grinning. "Sounds good. I'm getting tired of my own cooking. What time?"

"Five-thirty?"

"Sounds good." The doctor patted Holly's shoulder and shook hands with Ash, then left humming "I'll Be Home for Christmas."

"You should have told him your mom will be there."

"Maybe she will and maybe she won't. Last I heard, Harry might be taking her to dinner somewhere fancy."

"Really."

"Really."

The nurse entered pushing a wheelchair. Another followed behind her carrying a set of crutches.

Ash lifted Holly off the bed and settled her into the wheelchair.

"Is this really necessary?" she asked.

"Not only necessary," the first nurse said, "but mandatory, and I'll be pushing you all the way to the front door and to the curb, too."

"I can do that," Ash protested.

The nurse gave him a look. "I'm sure you can, big guy, but rules are rules, as you well know, since you're responsible for so many of our patients being here."

"Technically," Ash said, "I only coordinate their rescues. They are personally responsible for putting themselves in danger in the first place."

"He got you on that one, Denise," the second nurse

said, chuckling. "You can carry Holly's bag and the crutches, Ash. Unless they're too heavy for you."

"Hardy-har-har, Skyler," Ash said, even though he did laugh. "Be nice to me or I'll have Rock over here investigating you for harassing the fiancé of a patient."

"Please, do," Skyler said. "I'd love a personal introduction to the man of my dreams."

She said it so matter-of-factly, it took Holly and Ash a moment to realize she might be serious, not kidding.

Ash said, "Surely, you've already met Rock."

"I work for a living, unlike some people I could mention," she shot back, giving him the evil eye. "I don't have time to meet every visitor a patient has, you know." She sealed that proclamation with a wink at Ash before she left the room.

The other nurse said, "It's chilly outside. Let me grab my sweater and I'll be right back."

Holly glanced up at Ash. "You got a thing going on with Nurse Skyler?"

Ash laughed. "No! She and I went to the same schools, though she's about four years younger than me, and she's studying to be a Physician's Assistant. She also has a bigger mouth."

Holly managed to hold back a grin. "I'm not so sure about that."

He ducked down and kissed her, then asked, "Got a problem with my mouth?"

"Not in the least. I can hardly wait until you lavish me with a bunch more kisses all over my body." Holly wasn't sure where that brazen statement had come from, or how she'd gotten the nerve to utter it, but she wasn't sorry she'd said it.

She really *was* looking forward to him kissing her everywhere.

Rufus and Dinah

inah smiled down on Holly.

Rufus, on the other hand, aimed a frown down in her direction. "She should worry about her relationship with Ash and forget about matchmaking for her friends."

"I think it's sweet. Besides, isn't Grey next on our list?"

"We don't know that for sure," Rufus replied.

"Your glass is never half-full, is it, Rufus?"

"Certainly, it is."

Dinah gave him a look.

He *harrumphed* and said, "Well, I'm *mostly* a half-full glass kind of guardian angel."

She grinned. "Maybe in your dreams."

He scowled at her. "Okay, Knower of All Things, which man would Gina be suited to better, Grey or Rock?"

"She'd be fine with either of them, but Grey is the man she needs."

"Needs? Really? What about what she wants?"

Dinah pursed her lips, then said, "I'll bet you a hundred angel bucks that the moment she meets Grey, she'll want him."

Rufus gaped at her in surprise. "A *hundred*?"

"Too steep for you?"

"Did you win the jackpot at Guardian Angel Bingo or something?"

"Wouldn't you like to know?"

Rufus scratched his chin. "Frankly, my dear, there are a lot of things I'd like to know."

The sound of Dinah's delighted laugh sprinkled the sky with extra sunshine. "I had no idea you even knew how to read a book."

"Margaret Mitchell happened to be one of my charges back in the day," he informed her.

"Well, darlin', kiss my lips and call me Scarlett."

Chapter 22

The ride home was quiet, mainly because Holly fell asleep a block away from the hospital.

Ash pulled into the garage at his house, lowered the overhead door, and hopped out.

The door between the garage and the house flew open and Hank screamed, "Holly!" Behind him, Blaze barked with excitement.

Ash put a finger to his lips to quiet his son. "Holly's sleeping, Hank. Stay there, and keep hold of Blaze's collar so he doesn't trip me when I carry her in."

Hank nodded and his expression grew solemn.

Once inside, Ash debated where to lay her down, the sofa or his bed. He decided on the sofa. She slept on when he covered her with the throw.

Ash reached for Hank's hand and whispered, "No jumping in Holly's lap. She has stitches in her head and you could hurt her or make the stitches tear."

Hank nodded, his eyes on Holly. "How come her face is all purple and yellow?"

"Remember we talked about what it meant to be kidnapped?"

"Yeah."

"When the bad man took Holly, he hit her and it left bruises."

"Is that why she was in the hospital?"

"Partially, but she's okay now. Want to help me carry her stuff in?"

Hank nodded again, then whispered to Blaze, "You stay here and take care of Holly so no one kidnaps her again."

Blaze wagged his tail and smiled up at Hank, then put his head up on the sofa near Holly's face.

Satisfied, Hank said, "We better hurry, so she's not alone too long." He asked another dozen questions on the way to the truck, which Ash took time to answer.

Was it all kids or only Hank who asked the darnedest things?

When Ash and Hank returned, they discovered Holly was still sound asleep. Her guard puppy was sawing logs on the floor next to her.

"Are you sure she's gonna be all right?" Hank whispered.

Ash kept his voice low, too. "Grey says she will be, and we have to trust that he's right."

"A lady is here," Hank said. "She went to the cottage."

"A lady?" For the first time, Ash realized his son had been alone in the house. "You mean Lily?"

"No, a different lady. I heard your truck, so I came back."

"Hank, haven't we talked about you sneaking off?"

"Yeah, but this was 'portant. You were bringing Holly home."

Ash couldn't argue that, but still, he didn't like his son taking off without telling anyone. "Let's take a walk to the cottage."

"I'd rather stay here with Holly."

"Holly's sleeping. It's either go with me, or go to your room and stay there until I say you can come out."

Hank made his decision quickly. "Cottage."

Lily and a woman Ash didn't recognize came out of the cottage when Ash and Hank were halfway down the walk. Hank ran ahead to apologize to Lily for leaving without telling her.

"It's okay, Hank," Lily said, squatting down to speak to him face-to-face, "but don't do it again, okay?"

"Okay." He gave her a quick hug and ran back to his dad.

"Ash, this is Regina Freeman. She's s friend of Holly's, and also her attorney. This is Ash Hammell, Gina." She hesitated, but only for a moment. "He's the man Holly's going to marry."

"Marry?" Hank asked. "Like you and Uncle Sean?"

Lily nodded with a smile.

"So…Holly is gonna be my mom?"

Lily darted a look at Ash, who had a sneaking suspicion that she'd been talking to Olivia Strangewayes.

Gina extended her hand, eyeing him like she was the microscope and he was the gnarly amoeba. "Nice to meet you, Ash. Holly had good things to say about you."

He accepted her firm handshake, wondering if she was really Holly's friend.

Gina grinned. "Holly didn't mention me, did she?"

"No."

Her grin morphed into a laugh. "That sounds like Holly, all right." She clasped her hands in front of her. "You have a lovely place here."

"Thank you."

"Holly loves the cottage," Hank chimed in.

"I do, too. Holly is a lucky girl to live here."

"She's sleeping," Hank informed her.

Gina shifted her gaze from the boy to Ash. "Lily said there's been some excitement around here."

"I guess you could call it that," Ash said, still unsure about this Gina person's place in Holly's life. "Holly's ex kidnapped her."

Gina's amusement vanished faster than a jury could say, *Guilty*. "Is she okay?"

"He roughed her up."

Gina paled. "That bastard!"

Still angry over what Kingston had done, Ash went on. "She managed to escape, but fell into a sinkhole in the gold mine. She's been in the hospital for almost a week."

"Gold mine! Hospital! No wonder I haven't heard from her." She shook her head. "I was hoping I'd get here before he did, to warn her."

Too little, too late, Ash thought, looking for someone to vent his anger on. "Why didn't you call, if you knew about his escape?"

Gina took an involuntary step backward. "I just found out yesterday, and I did try to call her, but I kept getting her voicemail. Is she all right?"

She became so agitated, Ash felt obliged to reassure her. Even so, he stuck to the abbreviated version of what had transpired. "She's fine now, but she had a head injury and they had to remove a blood clot."

"Damn!" Gina looked down at Hank, who watched her with concern. "Sorry, Hank. I said two bad words and I shouldn't have."

"What's a bad word?" he asked.

"Never mind," Ash cut in.

Hank's gaze left Gina and went to his father. "What's a

bastard, Daddy?"

Ash knelt down so he could look into his son's eyes directly. "It's a really bad person, who does bad things to other people."

"Oh." He scratched his cheek. "So, the man who hurt Holly is a bastard?"

"Yes, buddy, and that's one of the bad words I don't want you using again, okay?"

Hank nodded, but his lower lip trembled, as if he thought he was in trouble. "What's the other one?"

Ash gathered his son in his arms and lifted him. "It was the word damn. I know you didn't know either of them are bad words, but now you do, right?"

A single tear dribbled down Hank's chubby cheek. "Right."

Ash could think of only one way to cheer up his son again. "Let's go see if Holly's awake, shall we?"

"Hurry, Daddy. She must'a missed me as much as I missed her!"

Ash opened the garage door, since Lily's car was parked in the driveway. "Thanks for watching Hank."

"You're welcome," Lily said. "Let me know if there's anything we can do for you guys."

He nodded and gave her a hug, watching until she pulled away before he closed the overhead door.

Inside, he closed the door between the kitchen and the dining room, hoping not to wake Holly with the drone of conversation between him, Hank, and Gina.

"Can we have peanut butter and jelly sammies?" Hank asked. He entertained Blaze by rolling a tennis ball on the floor for him to fetch.

"Sure," Ash said, glancing at Gina. "That okay with you?"

"Yes. I love PB-and-Js. Can I help?"

"Thanks, but I've got this." He gathered the food items and set to work making sandwiches. A few minutes later, the three of them ate a quiet lunch at the table, followed by a quick clean up. Hank fell asleep on the floor next to Blaze while Ash loaded the dishwasher. He finished what he was doing before he picked up his son and carried him to his room.

Back in the kitchen, he found Gina eating cookies she dunked into a glass of milk.

A knock sounded on the door between the house and the garage. A moment later, the door opened and Rock Dennison walked in, like he always did, because Ash had given him the code to raise the garage door.

Ash nodded.

Rock asked, "How's Holly?"

"Sleeping, as is Hank."

Rock glanced at the table and automatically flashed one of his killer smiles at Gina, who lost half her cookie to the bottom of her glass of milk.

Ash shook his head. Of all his friends, Rock was the one who had the ability to render a woman speechless with a smile. Too bad Rock didn't know that Gina wasn't the type of woman who would swoon over a man. She aimed a scowl at him and calmly reached for another cookie. "Rock, meet Gina Freeman, Holly's friend and attorney. Gina, this is Rock Dennison. He's a detective at Christmas Valley Sheriff's Office and also works for me at Mountain Search-and Rescue."

They exchanged a handshake, and if Ash wasn't mistaken, an unspoken truce.

The door between the kitchen and the dining room swung open and Holly came through, looking slightly dazed. "Gina?"

"Holly!" Gina shoved away from the table and the two women hugged.

Holly moaned a little in discomfort.

"Sit down before you fall down," Ash said. He pulled out a chair and helped her into it.

"When did you get here?" Holly asked Gina. "*How* did you get here?"

"Trust me, you don't want to hear how many plane changes I had before I got to my last stop and rented a car. Are you okay?"

"I'm a little wonky, but otherwise, I'm fine." Holly's gaze darted to Rock. "Do I know you?"

"He's the detective who helped rescue you," Ash said before Rock could speak, "and he also works for me."

Rock moved over and extended a hand to her. "Rock Dennison, ma'am. Glad to see you're doing better."

"Thank you." Holly accepted his handshake, then took a moment. "Are you here with an update?"

"Yes," Rock said. "I am."

Chapter 23

Rock removed his hat and coat and hung them on the hook by the door before he took a seat at the table. "Got any coffee?"

Ash nodded and poured him a cup. "Anyone else?"

"Yes, please," Holly said, as politely as if she were a stranger in his house.

Ash poured another cup and delivered both to the table. He slid into a chair and asked Rock, "Something new going on?"

"You could say that." Rock reached for a cookie, then looked at Holly. "Did Ash tell you Kingston was being arraigned this morning?"

"Yes." Ash had also told her the charges, which included kidnapping, aggravated assault, attempted murder, resisting arrest, and a few others the DA had thrown in for good measure. "I hope the judge didn't give him bail."

"His court-appointed attorney asked for it, but the judge denied it. Our sheriff, John Pulkinen, and the

Chuckawalla Valley State Prison were having a tug-of-war over who got the POS first. The sheriff wanted him to stand trial here before he was transported back to Riverside County."

Holly glanced at Gina, who wouldn't be sitting at the table if she hadn't known about Jarrett's escape from the California prison. "Why would he risk his parole by escaping?"

"I'm sure he never planned to be at the hearing," Gina said.

Holly frowned. "How did he escape, and why?"

Gina sighed. "Jarrett's problem is not his looks, but the evil that lives inside him. He sweet-talked the female prison librarian, and convinced her to have sex with him. She helped facilitate his escape from Chuckawalla, and now she's pissed that he ditched her." She glanced at Rock and back to Holly. "According to my source inside the prison, she's so ticked off, she gave them all the lurid details of their affair and Jarrett's plans."

"I don't understand. How'd he know where I am?"

"The librarian took their relationship seriously, and when Jarrett asked her to cozy up to Abercrombie Jones, she did it. Over pillow talk, she learned about me." Gina made a sound of frustration. "I had a break-in at the office right after you left town, but she and a friend of hers made it look like they were after my safe, not my records." She leaned forward and grasped Holly's hand. "It's my fault Jarrett got to you."

"That's not true, Gina. This is on him, not you."

Gina made a sound of distress in her throat. "You're too forgiving, Holly."

"There's nothing to forgive. Did you have any idea he'd want retribution so badly that he'd go to any lengths to find me?"

"No," Gina said, "but I *should* have known."

"Gina—"

"Don't try to make me feel better, Holly. I should have suspected he'd try something ahead of his hearing, and I should've removed any trace of you from my files." Gina stood up, looked around, and must have realized she had no place to go, because she sank back down and put her head in her hands.

"Now that you two have that settled," Rock said in a wry tone, "I'll cut to the chase. Jarrett Kingston's new temporary home is the county morgue."

Gina's head jerked up in surprise.

Holly stared at him in shock and disbelief. Had she heard right? "He's...dead?"

Rock nodded.

"But...how?"

"He ran at his arraignment and somehow managed to grab the court deputy's weapon. Mike Aaronson, who I work with at CVSO, happened to be outside the courthouse when Kingston barreled out with a hostage." Rock leaned forward, his expression grim. "It was Kingston's bad luck that Mike is a marksman. He took the guy down with one shot to the head."

"Oh, my God, that must have been horrible for the hostage," Holly said. "Is she okay?"

"She's fine, but only because she's Mike's cousin. She knew he was a sharpshooter and the instant he drew his weapon, she closed her eyes and went limp." Rock narrowed his eyes on her. "How'd you know he took a woman hostage?"

"That's the way he operates. He thinks women are weak."

"Here's hoping he rots in hell," Gina said.

"You're sure he's dead," Holly asked, feeling a little guilty because tears of relief streamed down her face.

"He's dead, all right," Rock said. "I saw him with my own two eyes before they transported him over for autopsy."

"Don't cry, Holly," Gina said, reaching over to hug her. "God works in mysterious ways and Jarrett has finally gotten what he deserves."

"I'm not sorry he's dead," Holly said. "It's just that…I don't want him anywhere near my baby."

Rock's expression went from grim to puzzled.

"Don't worry about that, sweetheart," Ash said in a gentle tone. "People like him don't end up in Heaven."

Holly wanted to believe him in the worst way. "I need to go home."

"You are home," he reminded her.

"To the cottage," she said for clarification.

"I can't keep an eye on you there and that was one of the stipulations Grey made before he agreed to release you, remember?"

Holly did remember, but Dr. Grey Dixon was at the hospital and she wasn't. What he didn't know wouldn't hurt him. He'd also said no sex for at least a week. If she stayed in Ash's house, and slept in his bed, she wouldn't give a damn about the one-week moratorium on their love-making. She'd want Ash's hands on her and his body on top of her and his baby-maker inside her. Still, it wouldn't hurt to sugar-coat why she wanted to go back to the cottage. "I have some catching up to do with Gina."

Ash's resigned expression told her he knew she was lying, but he didn't call her on it. "I'll walk you out to the cottage."

"No need," Holly said. "Gina can do it."

"Holly…."

She smiled at him. "We'll be back for dinner, okay? I'd like Gina to meet your mom."

"If she shows up."

"Yes."

"I invited Grey."

"I know."

Ash nodded. "We should cancel our plans to have

Thanksgiving at the inn tomorrow."

"Please, don't. I'd really like to go."

"Are you sure?"

"I am." Then she remembered. "Oh, no! I forgot that I promised to bring a dessert."

"Put a recipe in front of me," Gina said, "and I'll make it."

Holly nodded. Gina was a not only a good friend, she was also a great cook. "You're going to love the inn."

"I believe it," Gina said. "So far, you've been right on about everything and everyone here." She helped Holly stand and looked at Rock. "Are you having Thanksgiving dinner at the inn tomorrow?"

Rock smiled. "No, ma'am. Being the lone single guy at the Sheriff's Office, I'm working."

Gina shook her head. "I'll bring you a plate and you can fill me in on all the gory details Holly has left out."

"What kind of law do you practice back in your cushy office?" Rock asked.

"Estate law and I'm sick of it. All my clients keep dying." Holly laughed, but Gina delivered her punch line with such solemnity, it took Ash and Rock a minute to realize she was joking.

"I'll get your coat," Ash said.

Holly nodded. "Thank you for taking such good care of me at the hospital."

"All I did was sit by your bedside and hold your hand."

"That was everything I needed."

"Was it?"

"Yes."

He looked deep into her eyes. So deep, she thought he'd delved all the way into her soul. And then, he leaned down and kissed her.

Despite their audience, Holly slid her arms around his neck and kissed him back, which unfortunately reminded her that she was still recovering from the injuries she'd sustained thanks to Jarrett and the fall into the sinkhole. Her head began to spin and her body swayed. Her reaction might have been from the kiss, but she doubted it. She released Ash and grasped the back of the chair to steady herself.

"You okay?"

She smiled up at him. "Never better."

"You're a terrible liar," he said.

"Darn." She shot him a wobbly grin.

He shook his head and said to Gina. "Get the door and I'll carry her over to the cottage."

Before Gina could move, Rock stayed her with a hand to her forearm. "Grab your coat. It's cold out there."

Gina didn't argue. She pulled her coat off the back of her chair, then hurried over to the door. "What about Holly?" she asked.

Rock grinned. "Pretty sure the body heat between her and Ash will keep her warm enough for the short walk to the cottage."

He winked at her, which made Gina laugh.

Rufus and Dinah

Dinah twisted her hands together, fretting about Holly.
"Shouldn't you be thinking about getting over to the cottage?" Rufus asked.

"I *am* thinking. I don't need my darned hands to think!" she snapped.

"If you say so."

"Oh, go soak your head in bucket of water, Rufus."

"I've been thinking about what it would be like to be human."

His conversational segue threw her for a loop. "For heaven's sake! Now is not the time to have a conversation about that."

"Why not? Ash has control of the situation, and Holly seems perfectly content in his arms."

"Sometimes, you are so dense."

"I am not." He smiled down on the couple. Holly had her arms around Ash's neck and Ash had his strong arms tight around the woman he loved. "If anything, you're the one who's dense," he retorted.

"Why are we arguing about this?" Dinah demanded.

"I have no idea! You started it."

"*I* did? What dream were you in when *that* happened?"

"You said you didn't need your hands to think, when you know perfectly well that you talk with your hands half the time."

Dinah smacked his arm and zoomed off to the cottage.

"Why'd you do that?" he asked when he caught up with her moments later.

"Because I wanted to. Do you think a person who talks with their hands has to stop and think about what they're doing?"

"Well, yes."

"Well, you're wrong, Rufus. It comes naturally to me. Maybe eons ago, in another life, I was Italian."

Rufus roared with laughter. "That's funny, Dinah."

"I'll give you funny. What do you think the Big Guy is going to do to us if Holly and Ash are happy and satisfied with making love and don't get married by Christmas?"

"That's not going to happen."

"How can you be sure?"

"Simple. Ash reserved the Christmas Valley Inn for their nuptials."

"And when did Holly agree to marry him?"

"She…." He trailed off, startled.

"That's right! She hasn't said yes, and he hasn't bothered to ask her again. What do you think *now*, Mr. Know-It-All Guardian Angel?"

Instead of answering verbally, Fergus took the opportunity to silence Dinah with another kiss.

Chapter 24

Gina hurried ahead to open the cottage door with Holly's key.

"Give us a few minutes, will you, Gina?" Ash asked.

"Sure." Gina looked around, as if trying to figure out what to do with herself. She glanced toward the house and noticed Rock on the patio, with his phone to his ear. She headed back that way.

"Gina has good intentions," Holly informed Ash when the door closed behind them.

"I know."

"Why did you want her to leave us alone?"

"Because I have something to say to you, and it doesn't require an audience."

"Oh."

Ash kissed her again, then settled her into a club chair. He knelt down beside her and took her hands in his. "Will you marry me, Holly?"

Holly couldn't speak for a moment, even though he'd

asked her once before. When she found her voice, she mentioned a lingering concern. "We don't really know each other, do we?"

"We do in every way that counts."

Curious, she asked, "Such as?"

"You love my son."

She nodded.

"You're a good person."

"I try to be."

"We make excellent love together."

She smiled. "We certainly do."

"And you love me."

"I do, but even so, I don't understand any of this."

"What's to understand?"

"How can I be in love with you when we've known each other less than two weeks?"

"Some things are simply meant to be." He hesitated. "Besides, Christmas Valley is known for short engagements."

"It is?"

He nodded.

She smiled. "Are you going to wax poetic now?"

He smiled back, melting her heart. "If I have to."

"Are you sure?"

"About what?"

She shook her head. "You said Christmas Valley is known for short engagements. Is that really true, or are you pulling my leg?"

"It's really true, but if you don't believe me, I can bring in a dozen or so couples to back me up."

"Then, yes."

He cocked his head. "Yes, what? Going poetic or finding couples to confirm what I said or—"

"Yes, I'll marry you. Crazy or not, what I feel for you tells me…."

"Tells you what, sweetheart?"

"That you and I are meant to be together, forever."

"I agree." He kissed her again, careful not to hold her too tight and cause her more pain. "I love you, Holly. In spite of the short time we've been together, I know in my gut that what's happening between us is a forever thing, and I always trust my gut."

She laid her palm gently against his face. "That's the most romantic thing I've ever heard."

Ash must have thought she was teasing him because he said, "I wish I was better with words."

"Don't sell yourself short. You're terrific with words."

"I wish I could carry you off to bed and show you how much I love you."

"I wish you could, too, but Grey did say no sex for a week."

"Grey is full of you-know-what, but since he's the doctor, I suppose I have to defer to his judgment." He kissed her again. "I reserved the Christmas Valley Inn for our wedding and I asked Ryker to perform the ceremony."

"You've been busy."

"I'm in a hurry," he said, then added, "Not that I'm trying to push you into anything."

She leaned forward and put her forehead against his. "I wouldn't have said yes, if Jarrett hadn't died."

"I gathered that, but I had alternative plans to counter your resistance."

"Some day, you'll have to tell me about those. What's our wedding date?"

"Kris says they'll have the house and the property decorated by the first, in time for Santa's visit. I scheduled us for the fifth, which is a Saturday."

"I would've been okay with eloping."

"Yeah, but you're trying to get your Christmas spirit back, and I don't think eloping will do that."

"You really have covered all the bases."

He shrugged. "Gina will be your maid of honor, I imagine, and I already asked Rock to be my best man." He grinned. "Hank is excited about being the ring bearer, but he wants to know if Blaze can help him."

Holly laughed.

"What's so funny?"

"You! Never in a million years would I have pegged you for a wedding planner."

"Hunh. Are you trying to say I should step back and let the bride-to-be take care of everything?"

"I don't know about that. You're doing pretty well so far." She kissed him again, wondering if Gina would walk in, since a few minutes had long since passed. "Should I wear a white dress?"

"That's your choice, but I'd love it if you did."

"I got married in the judge's chambers before."

"Same for me."

"It wasn't how I imagined it."

"If Alicia hadn't gotten pregnant, I never would have gotten married, period, but it happened, and I've never been sorry I have Hank."

"He is pretty adorable, so I can see why, but regarding Blaze, he might have to sit this one out."

"Not a problem."

She bit her bottom lip. "Would you like more kids?"

"Absolutely."

A dark cloud settled over Holly. "After I lost the baby, the OB/GYN said I might not be able to have more children."

Without hesitation, he said, "I can live with that, but I can't live without you."

A knock preceded the door opening. Gina stuck her head in and asked, "Can I come in now? It's cold out here."

"She said yes," Ash announced in response.

"She would've been crazy not to," Gina said, grinning. "Congratulations!"

"I'm going make a colorful bride," Holly pointed out, "but maybe by then, some of my bruising will be gone.

Ash ordered three pizzas for dinner, all with different toppings. Gina volunteered to pay for dinner, so she answered the knock on the door.

Hank raced ahead of her to help.

Instead of a pizza delivery guy, Grey Dixon stood on the front porch holding three boxes from Pizza Palace.

"Hi, Grey!" Hank cried, waving and apparently happy to find both the doctor and the pizza at the door.

"Hey, buddy. How's it going?"

"Good, 'specially since we're having pizza for dinner." Hank rushed on, full of information. "That's my second favorite meal after sketti, which we were going to have except Holly got hurt and didn't feel like cooking. Grammy had a date tonight, so she's not eating with us. This is Gina. Daddy said you were coming for dinner, but I didn't know you'd bring the pizza!"

"I met the pizza delivery guy in the driveway," Grey said, handing the boxes over to Ash, who headed to the kitchen with them. "He told me he thought he saw Vixen and her boyfriend walk by just as he pulled in."

"Really?" Hank asked, standing between the doctor and Gina. "I gotta go look out the window and see if I can see them!" He bolted away.

Gina and Grey stared at each other for several moments without speaking.

Finally, Grey said, "We should close the door. It's cold outside."

"Oh, right," Gina said. "Wait! I need to pay for the pizza."

"I already did that."

"Why?" She backed up, but only because he stepped

over the threshold.

"Because I know Tony, Junior, and he forgot his coat, so he was shivering his butt off in the driveway, and I had plenty of cash on me to pay." He gave her a look. "Satisfied?"

"Who *are* you?"

"Grey Dixon. I'm Holly's doctor."

"Holly's doctor."

"That's right. Who are you?" he asked.

"Gina Freeman. I'm Holly's attorney."

Grey held out his hand. "Nice to meet you, Gina."

She looked down and debated accepting the hand-shake. "You, too."

"You gonna marry Gina, Grey?" Hank asked, back between them.

"Uh…," the doctor replied.

Gina shook her head and grinned. Poor Grey Dixon, silenced by a three-year-old. She glanced at Holly, who stood in the kitchen doorway. "They sure grow a crop of good-looking men here in Christmas Valley."

Chapter 25

Thanksgiving dinner at the Christmas Valley Inn was delicious and memorable, including the pumpkin roll Gina had made from one of Holly's recipes.

Everyone at the table was excited that yet another wedding would take place at the inn in a little over a week, although Hank might have been equally excited about meeting Santa on December 1.

By the time they left the inn, Holly knew who to talk to about a dress, the cake, the flowers, and her hair. She also asked about a caterer, because she wanted Kris and Nick to enjoy the event, rather than work through it.

Joss volunteered to set up appointments for Holly and Gina on Saturday. Holly agreed, but only because exhaustion from her ordeal still laid her a bit low.

Ash checked on her three times on Friday, and Hank came over twice with Blaze. How Gina occupied her time was a mystery, but she did let it slip that she'd had lunch with Grey Dixon. Holly found that interesting, because Gina and Grey had taken the promised food plate to Rock at the sheriff's office the night before.

By the time Saturday morning rolled around, Holly felt more rested. Doing absolutely nothing the day before except relax and sleep had been good for her.

She and Gina headed out at eight forty-five, with directions from Ash on how to get to Katydids on Ambrose Street. Lise Dennison, who was married to Rock's cousin. Ric, had a lovely selection of gowns appropriate for a wedding. Holly fell in love with the fourth one she tried on.

"OMG, Holly, it's perfect," Gina said, sniffling, "and I'm going to cry."

Holly turned in a circle, examining her reflection from every direction. "Do you think Ash will like it?"

"Ash wouldn't care if you wore a gunny sack," Gina said, then added, "Or nothing."

"Gina!"

"The woman makes the dress," Lise assured her, smiling. "This particular one, I designed, and I never imagined it could look this good on anyone."

Lily D'Arcy, her sister-in-law, popped in at that moment. "I just realized why I recognize you, Holly. You're Sophisti-Kitty, only you're ever so much prettier now that you're not model thin and you're back to your natural hair color."

"Thank you," Holly said, warmed by the compliment. "That's the past me."

"I take it you didn't like being a model," Lise said.

"I hated it. Grueling hours, prima donnas, fake people. Thank goodness I'm done with it forever."

"What are you doing now?"

"Freelance illustrations."

"Really." Lise considered her for a moment. "So, I could hire you to illustrate a catalog for me?"

"Sure."

"That's terrific! Let's talk after the holidays."

Holly smiled. "Perfect." She glanced at Gina. "What color would you like to wear?"

"I'm not sure. What do you think, Lise?"

Lise studied her for a moment. "I have a lovely emerald gown that could be shortened later to wear for less-special occasions. I also have a beautiful royal blue that would complement your curvy figure." She tapped her lips with her index finger, obviously thinking. "I have a red that would look amazing on you, too, and…never mind."

"What color is the never mind?" Gina asked.

"Silver, but you have to see it to understand, it's no ordinary silver."

"Silver is a Christmas color," Holly said.

"You're right. Shall I bring them all out?"

"Please."

Gina looked a little overwhelmed. "I had no idea being a maid of honor was so complicated."

An hour later, they were both fitted to their choices. "You can pick the dresses up on Wednesday," Lise said. "Your men won't know what hit them when they see you in these gowns."

"I don't have a man," Gina said.

"That's not what I heard," Lise said, which left Holly wondering who Lise had spoken to about Gina, and what she'd heard. Olivia Strangeways immediately came to mind.

Next they went to After Thoughts, a shop adjacent to Katydids. Gina was intent on purchasing something old for Holly to wear. As it turned out, Holly chose a delicate antique silver necklace with a heart pendant laden with tiny blue sapphires.

"Your dress is new and it just so happens," Gina said, "that I brought my sapphire earrings with me. You can borrow them."

Just like that, the something-old-something-new,

something-borrowed-something-blue was fulfilled.

Next, they headed to Carmen's Cakes. Ash had asked her to see if Carmen could do a chocolate cherry cake. Carmen said yes.

After that, they went down the block to Blooms-a-Plenty, where choosing bouquets and boutonnieres was made simple by Ava Cantore, who seemed to read Holly's mind.

Their next-to-last stop was Heads-Up, a hair salon. Stella Falconio examined both heads of hair with a critical eye, then sat Holly and Gina down and gave them each a trim, taking care not to cause Holly undue pain.

"Are you planning to wear a veil?" Stella asked Holly when she'd finished.

"No, but I would like something festive in my hair."

"Flowers or bling?"

"What do you think?" Holly asked Gina.

"Personally, I'd go with some classy bling," Gina said. "Flowers might get droopy."

Holly nodded. "I agree."

Stella offered up some ideas, then hurried two doors down to After Thoughts, and returned with several possibilities.

Holly held a mirror in her hand and examined the back of her head in the larger mirror. "My wound doesn't show too much, does it?"

"Hardly at all," Stella said, and Gina concurred.

They left the salon with only one stop left. Thirty minutes later, with new shoes now among their purchases, Holly was relieved that Gina was doing the driving. "I'm completely wiped out."

"You have time for a nap before dinner."

"I'm so tired, I might sleep *through* dinner."

"No, you won't. You and Ash are double-dating with me and Grey."

"And you didn't tell me this earlier because?"

"I wanted to surprise you?"

Holly shook her head. "I knew the moment you two met it would go somewhere."

"That's ridiculous." Gina took her eyes off the road for a moment to glance at her friend. "Did Ash invite him to dinner on Wednesday night for the purpose of meeting me?"

"FYI, neither of us knew you'd be here on Wednesday."

"So don't flatter myself, huh?"

"I didn't say that, did I?"

Gina grinned. "Tell me about the town psychic."

As it turned out, Holly fell asleep and no one had the heart to wake her when it came time to go out.

Gina and Grey went off to La Tavola for dinner without them and Ash used his key to get into the cottage, since Hank was spending the night at the D'Arcys again.

He shed his clothes and slid into bed beside Holly. He slipped his arm around her, content simply to be near her.

"Ash," she murmured.

"I couldn't stay away another minute," he whispered against her neck.

"I'm glad you didn't."

He pulled her a little closer and within minutes, both of them were asleep.

Ash wasn't sure how much time passed before he woke again. When he opened his eyes, he found himself staring into Holly's eyes. "What are you doing?" he asked, his voice raspy.

"Waking you up," she replied.

"How long have you had your hand…down there?"

"I just started."

"I was dreaming about you."

"Is that why you got hard so fast?"

He smiled. "You know Grey said no sex for a week."

"I don't have any broken bones, and I don't have any internal injuries, so I can't imagine why he would say such a thing."

"I don't want to hurt you, Holly."

"What if I promise to tell you if you if I'm in pain?"

With the moon half-full, and the blinds still open, her expression clearly reflected her intentions. "Can I trust you to do that?"

"I don't lie, or at least, I don't anymore."

"When did you?"

"When I went to work and stood in front of a camera. I hated every minute of it, but I had to pretend to love it. That was lying."

He kissed her with such tenderness, he almost couldn't believe it was him doing the kissing. "I'm sorry you had such an unhappy life."

"The past is the past. I'm looking forward to the future and the life you and I will have together."

"I am, too." He kissed her again and his hand wandered up under her pajama top to capture her breast."

"You can start there and we'll work up to the rest of it."

Still obviously conflicted, he eased away and pulled her knit top up and over her head, being careful not to disturb her stitches. "You're still so bruised."

"And you're still so hard."

He grinned with a slight shrug. "That, I can't help. It's all your fault."

"Good for me." She pulled his head down to her breast.

After that, nature took its course.

Rufus and Dinah

inah sighed, more content that she'd ever been before. "Rufus?"

"What?"

"Do you think what we just did was wrong?"

"No."

"You don't sound certain."

He sighed this time. "I suppose that's because I'm not." He glanced upward. "On the other hand, we would have heard a powerful roar of thunder from the Big Guy if we weren't supposed to do what we just did."

Dinah followed the skyward direction of his gaze. "I believe you're right." She stroked his chest with her hand, then moved it lower, toward the part of him that fascinated her almost as much as his mind did.

"Careful there, old girl."

"I don't really think of myself as old."

"Nor should you. It was strictly a figure of speech I picked up from my last jaunt in Merry Old England."

"You never told me how that turned out."

"As Shakespeare said, 'All's well that ends well.'"

"I was disappointed that the Big Guy split us up on that assignment."

"Me, too."

"I confronted Him about it, and you know what his response was?"

Rufus reared up off the puffy cloud that had served them well as a bed. "You did *what*?"

"I confronted Him, and why shouldn't I? We're supposed to be a team, aren't we?"

"Well, yes, but…what did He say?"

"'It's not yet your time.'"

"Dinah, please, don't play games."

"I'm not. That's exactly what He said. 'It's not yet your time.'"

"Curious, and odd."

"I don't know about that. I've given it a lot of thought and I think the Big Guy knew we were going to end up like this, but He didn't want it to happen back then, so he split us up when you visited your charge in England."

"Surely not."

"Bullpucky. He wanted it to happen now."

"Don't be daft, Dinah."

"No thunder, remember?" She gave his heavenly erection a little squeeze.

"Again?" Rufus asked.

"As Holly and Ash are likewise engaged, why not?"

"I'm up for it," Rufus said, his tone suggestive, "but first, I want to ask you…were you serious when you talked about becoming human?"

"Serious as the swine flu."

"Maybe we should make an appointment to talk to the Big Guy about it."

Dinah frowned. "I suppose we have to, since He's in charge."

"Would there be benefits to being human?"

"You know as well as I do that there would be."

"You're right. We could make love in a bed instead of on a cloud where anyone looking down from above can see us."

"Oh, dear." Dinah threw an arm over her heavenly breasts and placed a hand at the juncture of her heavenly thighs.

"Don't worry, I shielded us," Rufus assured her, "but I can't always guarantee that will work."

"Oh, dear," she said again, her eyes aimed upward.

"There's a tangible benefit I've thought about, too."

Dinah climbed on top of him and situated herself just so. "What's that?"

"We could have children."

"We would have to get married first."

"Yes, of course," Rufus said, though at the moment, his mind wasn't really on *having* children. It was focused, instead, on the part of his body that could *make* children if he and Dinah were human.

Chapter 26

Holly and Ash made love twice more during the night, but in the morning, she awoke to find herself alone in bed.

Had she been less in love, or less secure, she might have wondered where he'd gone off to. As it was, she had no doubts that Ash was still in the cottage.

Had Gina come in late the night before? Holly didn't want to streak around in her birthday suit looking for him, in case Gina was there. She pulled on her PJs, left the bedroom, and followed the scent of freshly brewed coffee to the kitchen. "Good morning."

He turned around smiling. "Good morning." His eyes raked her from head to toe and back up again. "You feeling okay?"

"I'm feeling better than okay. In fact," she said, sidling closer, "I feel like I could take on hours more of love-making."

His smiled widened. "I'd love to oblige you, but I promised Lily I'd pick up Hank by nine. The most we have time for is a shower, which has endless possibilities if we take it together."

Intrigued, she held out her hand to him.

He put down his coffee mug and took it, pulling her close for a kiss.

As for the shower, Ash proved he was a creative genius as he showed her what he'd meant by endless possibilities.

They went together to pick up Hank, who was glad to see them, though he was disappointed they hadn't brought Blaze along.

"We couldn't, buddy," Ash explained. "We're meeting Gina and Grey for breakfast."

"We are?" Holly didn't know why she was surprised, since Gina hadn't been in the cottage. "Did Gina come home last night?"

"I was too busy to notice." Ash gave her a smoldering look, which got Holly hot and bothered all over again.

"Where are we going?"

"Pancake Heaven. It's Hank's favorite place for breakfast."

"Yes, it is!" Hank cried from the rear seat.

Gina and Grey were already at the restaurant, seated at a large round table.

Hank hugged them, then let his dad lift him into a booster chair, though it was obvious he almost didn't need it.

"How was dinner at La Tavola?" Holly asked.

"Amazing," Gina said. "The food is delicious." She eyed Holly. "You look rested."

"I am," Holly said, and left it at that.

Gina cast a speculative glance at Ash, who returned her perusal with all the innocence of a choir boy.

"Where did you sleep last night?" Holly asked.

"At Grey's. He brought me back to Ash's place. I rang the doorbell, but no one answered, so I walked back to the cottage, but I didn't have a key, so…." She shrugged, unmindful that her cheeks had grown a little rosy.

Ash looked at his friend. "I didn't know you had a spare bedroom in your apartment."

"That's because I don't."

Holly couldn't contain a grin. The way the two of them couldn't keep their eyes off each other told her well enough how they'd spent their night.

Hank was over the moon that he got to sit on Santa's lap. He had a short list of wants for Christmas that included a baby brother, or a sister, if no brothers were available.

Santa had a good belly laugh over that.

Afterward, Hank stayed to play with the reindeer and after that, he got a personal tour of all the Christmas Valley Inn decorations, inside and out.

Holly and Ash headed into town to Six Window Williams.

"Funny name for a jewelry store," Holly commented.

"Count the windows."

Holly did. "Six."

"Hence the name."

Though Holly had her doubts, the store had an exquisite selection of wedding rings. An hour later, they found exactly what they wanted. Holly's ring was a gold band embedded with eight baguette diamonds. Ash had chosen a matching band, sans diamonds, with a Greek key design engraving around the outside.

"Are you sure you don't want two rings?" Ash asked, once they were back in his truck. "And more diamonds?"

"I love my ring," Holly said. "I love the simplicity of it and I love that it's gold, like yours."

He smiled at her. "I love you."

"I love you, too." She hesitated, then asked, "Do you think Nick and Kris would mind if we don't pick up Hank right away?"

"I'm sure they won't. What do you have in mind?'

"What do you think?"

Ash grinned and fifteen minutes later, they were in his bed.

On Friday night, Holly and Gina went out with Lily, Joss, Sylvie, Kris, and some others who were new to Holly, for a bachelorette night at FruityCakes. It was owned by two sisters, Charley and Stevie, who each had a set of triplets. Charley and her new husband, Tate, had a second set of triplets, and Stevie and her new husband, Spense, also had a six-month-old boy named Jake. Ash, Rock, and their friends had an equal-size bachelor party at Spanky's Poor Boy.

Holly and Ash planned to hook up afterward, but Gina and Grey put the kibosh on that. "No canoodling the night before the wedding," Gina informed them.

Saturday morning, Micah, Sean, and Rock arrived at seven a.m. to take Ash and Hank out for breakfast.

Holly and Gina packed up Holly's CR-V and headed to the Christmas Valley Inn at eight o'clock. Kris said later, it was the easiest wedding ever held at the inn.

The wedding march played over the whole-house sound system at eleven. Hank, looking cute in his pint-sized tuxedo, carried the satin pillow down the aisle with the rings on it. He smiled and waved at everyone as he went. No one would've guessed that he'd pouted the day before about Blaze being left out of the festivities.

Gina preceded Holly down the decorated staircase, dressed in a silvery gown that Gina had finally admitted that morning reminded her of Grey. Holly didn't ask for elaboration.

Holly descended the stairs, feeling more like a fairy princess than she ever had in any elaborate gown she'd worn in front of a camera. Her dress was fairly simple, though it was beyond beautiful, with a sleeveless, V-neck embroidery-and-beaded bodice and a flowing skirt. She carried a mixed bouquet of white flowers, with two red roses that matched Ash's boutonniere.

When she got her first glance of him in front of the fireplace, he nearly knocked her socks off. What the man did for a black tuxedo and a red cummerbund ought to be against the law.

She had no idea who all had come to the wedding. They were all Ash's friends, and soon enough, they'd become her friends, too.

Ryker Manning officiated beautifully and finally, he said to Ash, "You may kiss your beautiful bride."

Ash needed no second urging. In fact, he spent so long kissing Holly that she wondered what the onlookers must think.

He pulled away and said, "I love you."

"I love you, too."

He slid an arm around her waist and they turned to face their guests, smiling as applause broke out.

After they greeted everyone, Ash grabbed her hand and they stole away into a corner for another long and passionate kiss. When he pulled back, he asked, "How's that Christmas spirit thing coming along?"

She looked up at the man she loved and smiled. "Since I met you, I feel it more and more every day."

His dark eyes flared with desire. "I'm looking forward to helping you further your search."

"And I'm totally amenable to whatever you have in mind."

"How long before we can leave the reception?"

Holly laughed. "Kris said everyone will understand if we take off around two."

"Good. I have a surprise for you," Ash said.

"What?"

"If I told you, it wouldn't be a surprise, would it?"

"No. When can I find out what it is?"

"When we get upstairs. Give me five minutes before you follow me up to the bridal suite."

Curious, she slid her arms around his neck and kissed him. "I think the bride is the one who's supposed to steal away first."

"Trust me, in order to fully restore your Christmas spirit, we have to do this in reverse."

She nodded, eager to see what he had in mind.

Nick Kringle appeared out of nowhere. "Lunch is ready to be served," he said with a smile. "You two should probably take your seats."

"Bummer," Ash murmured, which made Nick laugh.

A little over two hours later, following a delicious lunch, an equally delicious chocolate cherry wedding cake, and a little dancing, Ash kissed Holly and said, "See you upstairs."

She nodded and watched him walk away. A quick glance at the mantle clock informed her she could follow him at two o'clock, straight up.

Holly chatted her way to the beverage table, where she requested two champagnes. A minute later, she made her way up the stairs holding two stemmed glasses in one hand. She used her other hand to lift her skirt.

The mantle clock chimed two. She knocked once on

the door of the honeymoon suite and entered. Using her backside to close the door, she scanned the darkened room. "Ash?"

"Over here." His voice was husky with desire and possibilities.

Holly set the flutes on the table to her right and locked the door. By the time she turned around, her eyes had adjusted to the vague light in the room. She kicked off her shoes and made her way to the bed.

Once there, her gaze slowly raked his beautiful body with appreciation. Her pulse quickened and her breaths came faster, knowing what awaited them together in that bed.

Ash favored her with a sultry smile.

Holly smiled back, eager to join him.

He wasn't completely naked. He wore a Santa hat on his head and a matching red stocking over his erection, which did little to conceal it.

"Any chance this gives your Christmas spirit the Holly jollies?" he asked, his tone hopeful and suggestive.

Holly reached over and pulled off the stocking, slightly amused and completely turned on. "Help me out of this dress and I'll show you how jolly I can be."

Ash laughed and came up off the bed so fast, she almost didn't see him move.

Moments later, her wedding gown lay in a puddle on the floor.

Their mutual amusement vanished. In its place came the most intense, tender lovemaking two people could share.

Holly finally understood what Christmas spirit was all about. She hadn't really lost it. It had simply been misplaced until Ash walked into her life.

Rufus and Dinah

Satisfied that their charges were now happily married, Rufus and Dinah sought out the nearest cloud, intent on doing exactly what Holly and Ash were doing on their wedding night.

"Tomorrow, when we report in," Rufus said, "let's talk to the Big Guy about our thoughts."

"We could do it today," Dinah said just as Rufus's hand moved down to her heavenly thighs. "But on second thought, tomorrow sounds good."

Author Note

This is my first Christmas Valley Romance with a single dad. Ash Hammell made a cameo appearance in *Jingle Bell Clock* and I've wanted to write his story ever since. Then along came Holly Morgan and *Holly Jollies* was born.

Speaking of Christmas, do you have favorite movies you watch every year? (For me: *The Bishop's Wife*.) Are there recipes you make for family and friends only at Christmas? (For me: ravioli and crazy soup.) Do you have special Christmas décor you can hardly wait to bring out? (For me, it's the tree.)

The closer we get to Christmas, the more I pray that families everywhere will be able to celebrate the holidays together. 2020 has been a horrible year. I hope in some small way, *Holly Jollies* has helped brighten it for you.

Many thanks to my editor, Nancy Jankow, whose dedication to helping me make my books the best they can be never ceases to amaze me. Nancy, who knew when we met all those years ago that we would be working together on my books?

In 2021, look for at least one more Christmas Valley Romance. Tentatively planned is *Yule Loge* (that's loge, like the upstairs in a movie theatre, not *log*, as in a tree). In the meantime, if you haven't read my other Christmas Valley Romances, I hope you'll give them a look.

May you have a blessed holiday season, and may 2021 be a year we want to remember with fondness!

Thank You!

Thank you so much for reading
HOLLY JOLLIES!
I'd love to hear what you think about it.
You can email me at
ann@annsimas.com, or post
a comment on my
Ann Simas, Author page on
Facebook. I hope you'll "like"
me while you're there, and if you are
so inclined, please leave a review on
Amazon.com, Goodreads.com,
or BookBub.com.

Just For Fun

If you'd like to submit a picture of yourself
reading this or any book by me, please
send your JPG to **ann@annsimas.com**
and I'll post it on my FAN page!

Available now, **HERE AND GONE**,
a Fossil, Colorado romantic thriller.

Turn the page for a preview.

HERE AND GONE

Chapter 1

Hannah Mason didn't actually move into her new home under the cover of darkness, but she might as well have, for all the subterfuge involved in her relocation.

That's what happened when you were a major front-page headline in the local papers for months on end. Hannah called it crucifixion by journalism.

In the beginning, it had been difficult to crawl out of bed and face the world. No one except her family got that she was immersed in grief. Outside, vigilantism prevailed and nothing short of burning her at the stake would have satisfied those who had assumed the role of judge, jury, and executioner.

If not for the diligence of that self-appointed lynch mob, she might have crawled under the covers and given up living altogether. Instead, being a woman of strong will and determination, she forced herself to get up, get dressed, and accomplish something every day, no matter how small the task or how difficult the effort to climb out of bed.

At first, that meant repairing the daily damage wrought by those who persisted in leaving hateful graffiti on her front door, or painted threats on her house. After almost a year, the entrance to her home had so many coats of paint, she gave up trying to conceal the messages and re-placed the door. Her brother-in-law installed a glass storm door over that, which she locked every night, and cleaned with a one-sided razor blade first thing almost every morning. There wasn't a nasty negative word in the dictionary that hadn't been used against her.

Regardless of the absurd lies and conjectures the media invented, or how many times the police pounded her with the same questions they'd asked a dozen times before, or who the life insurance company sent to interrogate her, Hannah refused to cave into depression or desperation. She also worked hard not to succumb to the grief that consumed her from the inside out.

After the vile defacements had been obliterated each day, she forced herself to sit at her home-office work station. As a scientific illustrator, she'd taken on jobs from various publishers and authors and, by God, she'd complete them. She called them her rejuvenation pills. She also made time every day to work on the book she'd started for Jay. Getting lost in line drawings and colorations had turned out to be an unexpected salve against the sorrow she experienced for her lost little boy every hellacious day.

When she couldn't keep her eyes open any longer, she tumbled into bed, hoping, praying, for a dreamless slumber. If she was lucky, she only cried herself to sleep. If she wasn't, she had nightmares about how horrific it must have been for Jason and Jay, her husband and five-year-old son, out there on the vastness of the Pacific Ocean, in a sailboat, all alone, with no one to rescue them from drowning when the boat capsized.

She tried not to think about the creatures that lived and thrived beneath the water and how they'd react to the temptation of human flesh.

She tried not to think about the dying thoughts of the two people she cared about and loved more than her own life.

And most of all, she tried not to think about how she would face the rest of her life without them.

Chapter 2

Hannah thanked God for the support of her siblings and their spouses. Without them, she might have gone crazy over the past two years, or given in to the haunting desire to join her husband and son in death.

Her sister Emily, six months pregnant, and her husband Craig, along with their brother Seth, and his wife Deena, had been instrumental in keeping Hannah's move and her final destination a secret. Much as she missed her parents, who had died before her marriage to Jason, she was grateful they hadn't lived to witness the lynch-mob mentality of the people they had called friends during their lifetime. The upside of them being in Heaven meant that her sweet little Jay had someone up there who loved him.

In conjunction with the move, Hannah had taken her illustrator *nom de plume* permanently, and backed it up with a legal name change. She clung to a wild hope that it would keep the media from tracking her down. For some obscure reason that she still didn't fully comprehend, they'd been so focused on denigrating and persecuting her with their words, they'd yet to discover her occupation. Both they and the police were under the mistaken assumption that she was nothing more than a rich housewife, bored with her husband and child. Even during the whole-house search, when the cops had torn out every drawer and emptied every closet, no one had ever questioned what she did with all the art supplies in her workroom.

The police hadn't found anything in the search, and

why would they? They were completely misguided about her being either rich or bored. Yes, Jason had earned a big salary, but neither their joint personal bank account, nor their joint savings account had held any funds at his death. She'd opened a savings account under her illustrator name before she and Jason had married and all her payments and royalties were direct-deposited. If he'd had access, that account probably would have been emptied, too.

Hannah found it odd that the other accounts had been cleaned out down to a dollar each, but she had attributed it to Jason's strange behavior for the last year of his life. She figured he had a gambling problem, since he'd gone frequently to Las Vegas, or maybe he'd adopted an expensive drug habit. Certainly, he was doing something he shouldn't have been during the evening hours he claimed to be at work. Otherwise, wouldn't he have answered his phone, or been at his desk when she and Jay had dropped in to bring him a surprise dinner?

Her husband had a small life insurance policy through his work and another, larger one he'd bought personally. She hadn't spent one cent of that one, but had taken five thousand from the smaller one as a cushion and put the remaining balance in the safe deposit box. With frugal budgeting, she managed to live comfortably on the money generated from the sale of her house and what she earned from her illustrations. The five-thousand-dollar cushion had yet to be touched.

In the overall scheme of life, what she needed most wasn't money, but a snuggle and a sloppy kiss from her little boy, and unfortunately, that was never going to happen again.

Hannah tried to shake off the dark cloud hovering over her. This was a new place. She had a new life. The daytime was for work. Nighttime was for climbing into her big, lonely bed, where she could spend all the time she wanted thinking about Jason and Jay, missing them so much it left her in physical pain.

She especially agonized over Jay's loss. Jay, who would never have a chance to be a teenager or a man or have a family of his own. God, she hoped Jason had wrapped his arms around his son to comfort him when they were drowning. She couldn't bear the thought of her boy thrashing about in the water, scared out of his mind, maybe even crying out for her to save him.

Little puppy claws clickety-clacked over the hardwood floors. Hannah forced the morbid thoughts from her mind and allowed herself to smile. She'd never had a dog before, and even though Bowie was still a pup, she was loving every minute of canine ownership. It would be even better when she got the golden retriever properly house-broken. He'd shown his intelligence already with his quick grasp of commands and his understanding of simple phrases, which gave her hope she wasn't simply cultivating a pipe dream about his smarts. "Ready to go outside?"

Bowie puppy-woofed.

Hannah grabbed her jacket. "Let's go."

Bowie raced to the door, but hadn't mastered the art of slowing down yet. He tried to put on his puppy brakes, but despite the belated effort, he slid the last five feet into the glass door. He yelped, as he always did, though he wasn't hurt, simply disgruntled.

Hannah laughed. These days, it was Bowie who kept her sane. What a horrible responsibility to thrust upon an innocent little puppy.

On Thanksgiving day, Hannah decorated a large Milk-Bone treat with a squirt of whipped cream from the Reddi-wip can in honor of Bowie's five-month birthday. For old-time's sake, she shot a squirt into her mouth, too.

Even after all these years, her mother's warning still came through loud and clear...and it still made her smile. *Don't squirt whipped cream into your mouths from the can. We're civilized, you know!* When her mom wasn't looking, her dad would sneak into the kitchen and join her and Emily and Seth in what her brother had dubbed The Forbidden Whipped-Cream Adventure.

Hannah had carried on the tradition with her son. Her heart ached remembering how Jay had opened his little mouth in anticipation of receiving the Reddi-wip squirt. They'd giggle and giggle and Jason would scowl and tell them only pigs ate directly from the container. It was one of the many grudges her husband had come to nurture against her. For the life of her, Hannah had no idea what had caused the nice guy she'd married to morph into a mean malcontent who seemed to take pleasure from hurting her.

Bowie yipped to remind her she was still holding his treat. Every day, the yips and squeals out of his mouth were sounding more and more like real barks. Hannah glanced down and said, "Happy almost-half-year birthday, Bowie."

Bowie's butt, and consequently his tail, waggled about a hundred miles an hour in response.

"Sit."

Like the smart dog he was, Bowie sat.

Hannah leaned over and held the treat out for him to lick. That done, she handed over the Milk-Bone, which Bowie promptly took over by the patio door. He loved to lay in the winter sunlight.

She repeated the Milk-Bone treat for the next six days, until the Reddi-wip can was empty. Not bad. Four days for a human and her dog to polish off a can of whipped cream. "Don't get too used to this," she said, handing Bowie the biscuit. "Thanksgiving only comes once a year."

His tongue came out and licked his chops in anticipation.

Hannah laughed. "You don't even know what I'm saying, do you?"

In response, Bowie gave her one of his sweet smiles.

It was almost time for their morning walk around the property. The pup chewed contently on the biscuit, occasionally glancing at Hannah. Once it was devoured, he jumped up and ran over to her, then back to the door.

Hannah slipped into her snow boots, then pulled on her coat and gloves. "You're in for a new experience today, Bowie. It snowed last night."

He announced his excitement over the prospect of meeting snow by dancing a doggie two-step.

"When we get back, I'm going to build our first fire."

He smiled up at her.

"Let's go."

Bowie ran to the family room, then back toward the door, nearly managing to stop this time before he crashed into it.

Hannah chuckled. "You've almost got it, haven't you?" She reached down and patted his head.

The dog nuzzled her gloved hand.

She opened the door and Bowie shot outside. He got as far as the edge of the patio, which was dry because it had a cover, and came to a screeching halt. He lowered his muzzle to smell the snow, then lifted a paw and tentatively tested it. In the next instant, he backed away, turning to glance at Hannah as he did so.

She pulled the patio door closed and took off running into the yard. Twenty feet out, she turned to see what was keeping her dog. His butt was firmly planted on the cold concrete patio. "Chicken," Hannah said, laughing. "Bowie, come."

He stood, but other than that, made no move to follow the command.

"Bowie, come!"

This time he stepped gingerly into the snow, decided he liked it, and went down on his belly, licking the wet stuff as he crawled toward her.

"I'll go without you," Hannah threatened.

Bowie apparently didn't care. He rolled over and wriggled around on his back. Talk about a quick attitude conversion.

"Bowie, *come!*"

With obvious reluctance, he got up on all fours again and took a tentative step forward, and then another, and the next thing she knew, he was loping through the six-inch layer of snow, puppy-yipping for all he was worth.

Hannah laughed again and continued on toward the back of the property. Familiar with the route by now, she knew she wouldn't encounter anything beneath the snow to trip her up.

Bowie frolicked alongside her as she climbed the gentle slope. At the top of the hill, he went off to take care of business under his favorite tree. Five minutes later, he came back to her, cavorting like the puppy he still was, amusing her with his antics.

Half an hour later, they were back at the house. Hannah dried him off on the patio, including his wet little paws, before she let him inside. He thanked her with a generous lick.

She removed her boots outside the door, then took those and her coat to the mudroom, where she deposited her boots in the boot tray to drip dry. Her coat went on the last hook of the rack and her hat and gloves in a basket hanging from the first hook.

Not for the first time, Hannah marveled at the differences between beach living and mountain living. She'd never seen snow in person before moving to Fossil, so she and Bowie had that first experience in common. The snowman she'd built up on the hill, with Bowie's help, was no Frosty, but she'd have plenty of time to learn the proper way to make one.

Next on the agenda, breakfast. She put together a casserole using Italian sausage she'd browned and crumbled the day before, green chiles, grated cheddar, and eggs. While it baked, she put her boots back on and went out to get firewood. Whether it was ridiculous or not, she'd been waiting for the first snow to build her first fire. She found herself almost giddy with excitement.

After that, she walked out to the mailbox. Not that there would be anything other than bills, but she didn't want the mail carrier to report to authorities that she must be dead because her mailbox was stuffed full. Company, or anyone wearing a badge, was the last thing she wanted at her door.

Back inside, she made a pot of coffee, checked the timer on the oven, and went to her office to boot up her laptop. Emily sent her an email every morning, usually with a picture of her pregnant self. Today was no exception, if the little paperclip beside Em's name was any indication.

Hannah didn't eat while she was drawing, but she usually took her breakfast to her laptop to read the few emails she got and the day's news. She deleted three junk transmissions, read one from the editor she worked with at a publishing house, replied to a query from an author who was indie-publishing a children's book, and finally, it was time to read Emily's. She resisted looking at the attachments first. How much could her sister's belly have grown in one day, anyway?

Hannah,

I tried to call you last night and this morning, but your phone goes directly to voice mail. Please, please, please, since you insist on living in the wilderness, at least keep your phone on and charged if you're not going to check your email regularly!

Craig just returned from his East Coast trip. The way airlines are these days, with all the bumping and overbooking, he got bumped and had to take a different flight home, which necessitated changing planes in Denver to catch the flight home to San Diego.

Hannah shook her head. Emily always did take the long way around a story.

You may be wondering where all this is leading and all I can say is, I wanted you to understand how Craig came to be in Denver, but didn't stop to call or see you. He only had a 30-minute layover and he missed his connecting flight because the first leg was late. He tried to get another one, but at that point, they said they had nothing else available until morning. He was pissed, but he went out to catch a courtesy bus to a nearby hotel because he didn't want to sleep in the airport. He was waiting at the curb, when he got a call from the airline that they were going to get him on an 7:20 p.m. flight out, after all.

Before you read further, open the attachments I sent, then come back and read my second email.

em

Hannah's mouth twisted in a wry smile. Her sister could be such a drama queen. She put down her breakfast and used the mouse to open the first attachment.

Shock immobilized her. Instead of Emily's pregnant belly, up popped a picture of Jason. Although he sported a short beard, there was no mistaking him. Hannah enlarged the photo, then grabbed her magnifier to examine it more closely.

It was Jason, all right, unless he had an identical twin he'd never mentioned.

Or, it could be that she was losing her mind.

She jumped up and went to grab her cell phone, which was on the kitchen counter. She turned it on, on her way back to the workroom, where she opened the second attachment. Again, she stared at the photo, stunned.

Jason, Jay, and Sabine. How could that be? Jay looked older, which didn't compute with her memory of how he'd looked nearly two years before. Besides, how could that be, unless....

Unless he was still alive. Then, of course, he would be older. Had he lived, Jay would be almost seven now. And what was Sabine doing in the picture? She'd left San Diego a couple of weeks before Jason had taken Jay out on that fateful boat ride. Hannah had missed her friend terribly during those dark days when everyone else, including her neighbors, had treated her like a pariah.

She enlarged the photo and took the magnifier to it. There was no question. It was Jason with Jay and Sabine. Her mind was intact, but the facts in front of her didn't make sense.

She'd never seen Jason with a beard and though Jay was older, she still recognized him. Was this some good-intentioned effort on Craig's part to help make her feel better?

Her breakfast forgotten, Hannah hit speed dial for Emily. Instead of a greeting, she went straight to it. "What the hell is going on?"

· · ·

HERE AND GONE
A Fossil, Colorado Book #1
Available worldwide in paperback or as an ebook at
amazon.com

Also available in paperback from
annsimas.com

About the Author

Ann Simas lives in Oregon, but she is a Colorado girl at heart, having grown up in the Rocky Mountains. An avid word-lover since childhood, she is the author of 33 novels, one novella, and seven short stories. She enjoys writing, especially cross-genre books that are a mix of mystery–thriller–suspense, with a love story and more often than not, paranormal or supernatural elements.

In addition to being a three-time Romance Writers of America Golden Heart Finalist, Ann is also an award-winning watercolorist and budding photographer who enjoys needlework and gardening in her spare time. She is her family's "genealogist" and has been blessed with the opportunity to conduct first-hand research in Italy for both her writing and her family tree. The genealogy research from century's-old documents, written in Italian, has been a supreme but gratifying and exciting challenge for her.

Contact the author via:
Magic Moon Press
POB 41634
Eugene, OR 97404-0386
or at **ann@annsimas.com**

Or visit:
annsimas.com *and*
Ann Simas, Author on Facebook
Ann Simas on BookBub.com

Ann's books are available worldwide at
amazon.com

Made in the USA
Las Vegas, NV
23 November 2020